BEHIND THE 8 BALL

BEHIND THE 8 BALL

by

DAVID TEMPLE

Published by St Simons Press

ST SIMONS PRESS
601 West 57th Street, Suite 30-Q
New York, NY 10019-1380

ISBN: 978-0-9891865-8-2 (eBook)

ISBN: 978-0-9891865-7-5 (Paperback)

Images by Google
Editorial by Tammy Scott & Faith Fisher
Cover & book designed by David Temple
Published & manufactured in the United States of America

CONTENTS

BEHIND THE 8 BALL

a Carter Matheson Novel

Also by David Temple:

Discovering Grace
Stealing Hope
Lucky Strikes

This story is dedicated to all the brave men and women of our Armed Forces who step into harms way every day and put their lives on the line so that we may live under the canopy of freedom.

Thank you to friends & family who encouraged me through the long writing hours of the NaNoWriMo Competition. Special thanks to Tammy Scott who was always present to provide me an *extra push*.

Freedom is never more than one generation away from extinction. We didn't pass it to our children in the bloodstream. It must be fought for, protected, and handed on for them to do the same, or one day we will spend our sunset years telling our children and our children's children what it was once like in the United States where men were free. —*Ronald Reagan*

Our Mission Operation Nicaragua, or OPNIC, as our team had abbreviated it, had proven to be a very successful mission in Nicaragua and nearby Costa Rica. With the assistance of my longtime pal and former military compatriot, Steve "Mack" McKenzie, we were able to bring Dr. Leonard Caprese to justice. That feat was essential for any number of reasons, not the least of which was finding the hole in the proverbial bucket—a vessel of information that had been leaking for some time and causing not only momentary bursts of chaos, but did nothing to support the fortress of top secret information that our government held so close. Caprese was originally one of the good guys, but because of greed and lust for power—two of the most timeless and classically devastating of all obsessions, he had dipped his toe into the camp of the enemy. Using relationships he had built while working in the Department of Security, he systematically became obsessed with gambling with America's safety, all in the name of position. His modus operandi was to posture himself as an essential link of the safety chain of America's fight against terrorism. While seeking to play one against another, his warped thinking allowed him to feel like he was helping his country by bartering his highly protected information—that being the President's location during one of the most highly publicized, and consequently, extremely exposed meetings of the most powerful leaders in the world. This bargaining chip was in exchange for secrets to the location of terrorist rebels. It wasn't an altogether ridiculous proposition. In fact, he was gaining a front row seat to one of the more coveted of all terrorist information. His ally, one Asghar Debashi, was a traitor himself, playing both sides of a very dangerous fence. Debashi was killed in an ambush, when Mack and I, along with two of our allies David Morrison and Jake Cantor assisted in storming Caprese's behemoth compound overlooking Salinas Bay, just shy of the border of Costa Rica. Both Debashi and his executive assistant and business partner, Bernhard Devereaux were killed during the assault. The rest of the entourage turned out being five accomplices: David and Jake, along with my father—a latecomer to the party, along with his business partner and part-time bodyguard, Mr. Black. Rounding out the colorful entourage was my recent ex-girlfriend, Stephanie, a highly skilled surgeon from the Wilmington, NC area. She had come along for the ride; perhaps it was because of adventure that was lacking in her life. It could also have just been that she was missing me; either way, in harms way was no place for her to be. And by the same token, I was happy to have seen her.

While it felt like a month as we were enjoying it, the week came to a close much too quickly. Stephanie, Mack and I had genuinely unwound. I suppose it was the first time I had done that in a very long time. And we did so by doing pretty much nothing. We fished, swam and napped, on and off, for the entire time. Whether we were lounging on the deck, swimming in the ocean, or scuba-diving with locals, we truly unplugged. We were thinner, fitter, and tanner than we had been in years. We were ready to face the world again. Mack and I spoke very little about work; that was one of the rules set forth by Captain Stephanie, early on. Even she kept all work chatter to an absolute minimum. In fact, the only thing she spent any time talking about was the possibility of providing her medical services to parts of the country, most of whom were not as advantaged as the United States. I was impressed, because she's the most driven woman I've ever known. Seeing her this relaxed and present, made me rethink things with her; it made me realize just how much I enjoyed being around her. However, knowing my lifestyle, and the inherent dangers that went with it, that reality made me return to that place of doubt. Things will be what they're going to be, I thought to myself. Just enjoy the ride.

Stephanie, Mack and I arrived at Dulles International Airport, via the company's private jet, at daybreak, having orchestrated a red-eye out of Liberia. Mack and I felt an obvious void that we weren't going to debrief with Jerry, as we did with every mission. Here, Mack would catch a commercial flight bound for Savannah. Stephanie would do the same, heading back to Wilmington then drive down to Wrightsville beach. She was going to try and make her rounds around midday. The time had come to get back to reality, so we all said our goodbyes, hugged and waved one another off, all going in opposite directions.

After they left, I headed back downstairs where I grabbed the same private jet we just flew in on—one of the perks of being the big dog on campus. We were gassed up and pulling away from the hangar when I decided to open my laptop for the first time in over a week. The flight would only take an hour and I thought it best to do any business I had before I got home. Sipping a cold beer, I opened the laptop and started importing photos of our boating expedition from my iPhone. I'm gonna miss those two, I thought, watching the photos import, one by one, onto the laptop. Might as well check my email too, I thought. An alert popped up on my screen telling me I had an urgent message being sent via secure email. I punched in my security code and waited for it to connect to our secure servers. The next image that appeared on my laptop was startling and one that—whenever it appeared, was rarely good news. I took a deep sigh and thought, looks like it's time for the next mission.

1.

THE NEWS

SUNDAY, MAY 2 — 0711Z (This is 7:11AM/Zulu or GMT, Greenwich Mean Time)

The clandestine email that just arrived, dated one week ago, was coming from Jerry's office. That's the day we captured and killed Debashi and hauled the traitor, Dr. Leonard Caprese, off to prison. The subject line read: URGENT - Your Eyes Only. After an additional step of necessary encryption, the following message appeared:

(April 25 - 0415Z) — ATTENTION: Captain Carter Matheson, US Army — This message is to alert you that according to our latest intel, your father, Lieutenant Colonel Randall Matheson, US Marine Corp, has been reported as Missing In Action. According to sources within our bureau, approximately 0100Z, after departing Costa Rican airspace, our office was alerted that they lost contact. Lieutenant Colonel Randall "Bulldog" Matheson, Sergeant Thomas "Tommy" Black and Jennifer "Xeon"

Black, along with co-pilot, Officer Daniel "Spike" Jefferies, were all reported as missing when they did not arrive, as planned, to Miami International Airport. The group was scheduled to arrive 2 hours and 45 minutes later, after an estimated departure time of 0104Z. The estimated arrival time was approximately 0352Z. We understand you have been out of reach for the past several days, but we need you to contact our office immediately upon your return. Lieutenant Colonel Matheson's wife has been contacted, as well as Sergeant Black's wife. Please accept our sincere condolences and rest assured that we will leave no stone unturned before we find these four officers.

Sincerely, Sergeant Major Daniel Whitestone, USMC

I closed the laptop and felt my stomach drop and peripheral vision narrow. My palms began to sweat and I could feel the pulse quicken under my scalp. What the hell? What in God's name happened to Dad? What happened to ALL of them? I wanted to scream. Actually, what I really wanted to do was hit somebody, or some thing. My mind began racing, trying desperately to put the pieces together. I took a deep breath, shut my laptop down and closed my eyes. I had to concentrate. THINK, dammit!

I began replaying the events of that last night together. Randall arrived and we went to the motel. He debriefed us then we proceeded right to our lookout point above the Caprese compound. I went down with Mack, ordering Dad to stay back. I lost contact with him from that point until he piloted the helicopter onto the front lawn.

As soon we all said our goodbyes, he and Black and Xeon—WAIT! That's right, they were taking Caprese back to DOQ before popping over to San Jose and flying out of there.

No! They were flying out of DOQ. Wait a minute, Daniel Oduber Quiros is an international airport. They wouldn't have to fly out of San Jose. So, WAS Caprese left with authorities there? Or, would he travel back to Miami with Dad—then catch a transfer to DC?

As my mind raced, I don't recall hearing exactly how Caprese was going to get back, or to whom he was being entrusted. Shit! I opened my laptop in order to read the letter again. No mention of Caprese. That's strange. But then that would tell me that he was NOT on board that flight. I had to find out where Caprese was headed, who had him and when was he scheduled to depart DOQ. There's nothing I can physically do until we get there. I checked my watch. We had another 20 minutes or more. I'll call the minute I land.

I landed safely in Charlotte, grabbed my bags, found my truck in a parking lot several miles away and started for home. It was good to be back in North Carolina, and I picked up where I left off with my life, like I usually did. The message from the Bureau shifted my world though.

While my father and I were often at odds—over any number of things, I still loved and respected him. He had been a bulldog most all his life; thus, the nickname, but at the end of the day, he loved his family and his country more than anything in the world. There had to be a reason he went missing.

You don't just board a plane and disappear into thin air, I thought.

There had to be an explanation, and I was going to move heaven and earth to find him. Right now, I needed to reacclimatize myself to "normal" and regroup my thinking. I'd made all the necessary calls on the plane and no one knew anything more than the email that was sent to me. So, for the most part—at least for the next several hours, I would take a deep breath, grab a bite to eat and plan my next moves.

Back at home, I made a pot of coffee, as I did every morning, then spent the next few minutes catching up on only the essential of daily headlines. I fed Samson, my chocolate lab, and went out the back to chop a chord of wood. I'd learned a long time ago that if I did even a bit of vigorous exercise every single day that I'd remain fit and feel better. I also slept better; not to mention the fact that if you like to tilt a few from time to time, like I do, then it helps keep the waistline in check, as well as the rest of my body.

After grabbing a quick shower, I headed into town to grab breakfast at The Derby Diner, a local joint that's been operating since the '50's and hasn't changed much at all since then. I ordered the same thing I always do, while sitting in the same booth that I always did. Routine is a good thing.

Mission Grove is a handsome little community about 45 minutes outside Charlotte. It's just big enough to have all you need, but small enough to feel like family. It's a place I grew up and where my brother and his children live. This part of the country is beautiful and I most enjoy being in the mountains, just outside Asheville—another hour further up the road and set between the Blue Ridge and Great Smoky Mountains. While most of my time is spent on missions that take me all around the world, there's nothing like coming back home again.

It was time to get down to the business of finding Dad, so after breakfast, I drove back home to start the next phase of what was beginning to feel like a continuous journey. I rang Randall's wife and we spoke for nearly a half hour. She was obviously upset, but was taking his disappearance better than I had expected. After the initial shock of the conversation, we got caught up on life. About the time we drifted into recalling fond memories, it started to feel as though we were talking about him in the past tense, so I started wrapping up by telling her I'd be in touch and keep her apprised of any developments, no matter how large or small in detail. She thanked me, reminding me it was my turn to visit and finally, and after a number of goodbyes, we hung up.

The next call I made was to Mr. Black's wife. Lauren was practically nonplused. It wasn't that she was callous or didn't care; it was more that her life was lived knowing that at any time something like this could or likely would happen. I found that sad, as it didn't allow much confidence that Tony was the best in the business. As a Sergeant, he had enough credentials to be doing anything in the force that he wanted to, but instead chose to resign himself to being what several said behind his back was nothing much more than an Executive Assistant. Tony shrugged it off knowing that most people were jealous. The reason being that he was making nearly double what he made while in the Corp, but didn't have to answer to anyone except my father. And lastly, given that Tony still had a taste for action, he was able to travel all over the world and step into shit from time to time. And it was the kind of shit that we all long for. After all, that's why we joined in the first place. Mrs. Black and I likewise made small talk, and while she was a very bright bulb—graduating in the top of her class, Lauren was about as interesting as a pair of socks. We finished up, I hung up and then dialed up another call. Next on my list was Jennifer's roommate. Jennifer, or rather, Xeon, lived with a University student in Miami.

Never could figure out where Xeon got that name. I figured she just wanted to be different, or to be recognized. With the uniqueness of her heritage, along with her figure—nearly six-foot, quite buxom and beautiful as hell, it was hard not to be recognized, or seen as different. Mission accomplished, I thought. I got her roommates number from the Bureau and dialed it. No answer. After leaving a short message and offering innocuous details so as not to frighten her, I hung up and considered my next move.

My third call was certainly going to be the one that brought me the most grounded feeling. I grabbed my phone and rang the only person I could imagine would have an idea of what we would do to relocate LT. He picked up before the second ring.

"Wow, that was fast," I said.

"Miss me already?" Mack asks. "It hasn't been 24 hours. Isn't the rule you have to wait at least a week before you call after the first date?"

It was not only a funny line to open a conversation with, but the high-pitched voice he used made it all the more hilarious. We made a few paragraphs of small talk about the flight home, how much fun it was being on the gig together, and how beautiful Stephanie was after all these years. I agreed to all his points and then proceeded to cut to the chase.

"Bro, I need your help."

"Wasn't getting shot at and nearly killed a second time

enough for ya?"
After my unremarkable chuckle and too many seconds of silence, he knew something was up and asked, "What is it?"
"It's Dad," I said.
Mack was silent for all of five-seconds and then spoke quietly, showing no desperation, "Talk to me."
"He's gone missing."

2.

THE CALL

SUNDAY, MAY 2 – 0715Z

The silence on the phone was so quiet I could hear my heartbeat. My pulse was only slightly elevated. I knew exactly what Mack was thinking and how he was feeling. Angry, just like me. I'd give him another moment or two to process things, because I knew he would do the same thing I was. First, he'd replay in his mind exactly how the events of that last night ended—running a checklist to see if there were any loopholes that we were missing. Secondly, he—like I, would go straight to orchestrating all the details as to how we were going to find him. It shouldn't be difficult. After all, both of us were hunters.

"Okay, buddy," Mack said, choosing a deliberate tempo. "Not a problem. Just hang in there. We're gonna figure this out. We will find him. That's what we do."

This was Mack remaining calm, wanting to put me at ease, but we knew one another well enough that ease was not a place I chose to be very often. Moreover, he knew that I would have already run all the things his mind was mentally building.

"I know, pal. That's why I'm calling you," I said, patting my pocket for a cigarette. Nothing. "Let's reverse engineer this thing," I added, scanning the kitchen counter and dining room table.

I spotted my smokes on the edge of the fireplace mantel, lit one and waited for the nicotine to dull my nerves.

Mack got right to specifics. "Okay, so David and Jake took off to their next gig. Randall, Mr. Black, daughter Xeon and Caprese were the only ones supposed to be on that flight."

"Copy that," I said, releasing a long stream of smoke.

"Who was scheduled to fly them out? If they're within ten feet of your dad, we'd know who they were," Mack said, stopping to consider the team who would be on standby for that flight.

"Exactly. So, it has to be one of his cronies out of Miami," I said, scratching my overgrown goatee. "Either that, or someone out of DOQ in Liberia. But..."

"But we never fly with pilots we don't know," Mack interrupted.

"Unless all hands are on other decks. Or, if the matter is particularly time sensitive. Or, it's last minute—like this was," I added.

"Right."

I took another drag off my cigarette, tossed it in the fireplace and went to the kitchen to get a soda. I needed a shot of carbonated sugar. I pulled a ginger-ale from the fridge and headed out back.

"You still there?" Mack asked.

"Yeah, just needed some fresh air," I answered, adding, "You know what my gut says?"

"Huh?" he grunts.

"My money's on the fact someone slipped in at the last minute. And because it was late and LT was exhausted and ready to get back to dump our perp..."

"They let it slide," Mack interrupted.

"Think about how easy it is to look the part. Not to mention you have the distraction of international protocols..."

"And that amazon, Xeon," he chuckled. "Like you said, everyone was toast and just wanted to bounce."

I caught myself pacing from the woodpile to an enormous oak that had been shading this property for nearly a hundred years. I squinted as the sun shimmered off the pond. Something felt funky and I couldn't put my finger on it.

Mack was rustling on the other end of the line, when I asked, "What are you doing?"

"What do you think?"

A hawk flew overhead at that moment and let out a cry. It dove into the tall thicket surrounding the pond, snatching a rodent that had exposed himself too much and trying to retreat too late.

"What?" I asked absently, watching the hawk return to a tree high overhead.

"I'm packing. Getting ready to come help you find LT & Company."

"You know that has to be it, right? LT's guy arrives, all gassed up and ready to fly, when someone—or someone's...steps in and hijacks the bird."

Mack snorts, "No shit. The one thing we know about

Caprese more than anything else is that he has the means—both financial and personnel, to orchestrate anything he wants."

"True. Look at how long it's taken for us to catch him."

"Years," Mack mumbles.

"Right. So, what makes us think any of this shit was going to be easy? Meaning, even if we were able to locate his hideout, intercept his next plan of action...he would still have a Plan B, right?"

"Yep."

I let our discovery sink in a few minutes before looking up into the trees to see what progress Mr. Hawk had made with Mr. Rodent. Shielding my eyes from the sun, I saw Mr. Hawk licking his talons, enjoying the last tasty bite.

"Hey, you ever notice how Caprese has two of everything?"

"How's that?" Mack asks.

"Two homes: one in DC and one in Nicaragua. Two bodyguards, in both homes. And he holds, or rather held, two offices in the White House..."

"While working two sides of the fence," Mack interrupts.

"Exactly. And, you know that a man of his...precision and planning would have a backup."

I could feel Mack on the other end getting heated. And the next outburst confirmed it.

"Hell, I wouldn't even put it past that fuck to have planned to get caught—just so he could declare a cleaner getaway."

"Bingo," I said, scouring the back of my mind for specifics. It sounded a bit convoluted, and may not be entirely right, but one thing was for certain: we knew LT and company was missing, Caprese was outside our reach and we had to move instantly if we were to relocate, retrieve and re-imprison the bad doctor.

"Mack, don't forget," I added, "We both know that if someone's not found inside 24 hours..."

"The chances get mighty slim of finding them," he adds. "Boss, I can be packed and on a plane inside the hour."

Checking my TAG Heuer watch, I calculate a few steps and say, "Ditto, but it'll take you two."

I was already in the house, dumping dirty clothes from the last trip and tossing clean ones into my overnight bag.

"Tell you what; it'll take the same amount of time for me to fly to you, or you to me. So, let's call it 3 hours and rendezvous in Miami. We need to get there to sniff around anyway. Sound like a plan?"

"Done 'n dusted."

I chuckled, asking him where he got that term—something I hadn't heard him use for a really long time. He went on to explain how an English flight attendant he met on his recent trip home had used it. It meant something that was completely finished or understood.

We hung up, I packed up then rang up DC to order a private bird in Miami. Both Mack and I would land at MIA before cocktail hour and would have to design our POA to find LT and company—all of whom were in a different sort of MIA. I knew one thing: The clock was ticking and we had to move fast. Again.

3.

THE SWITCH

SUNDAY, MAY 2 — 1007Z

Dr. Leonard Caprese wasn't one for sitting around and waiting for things to come to him; he had always been a man of action. Even when it didn't look as though he was doing much, his mind was always racing. And at this particular moment, that was once again the case.

Caprese was flashing back to early childhood. The feelings of abandonment still stung regardless of the fact that it was nearly five decades ago when he learned that his birth mother and father dropped him off at an orphanage to let someone else care for him. Because of handsome looks, quiet demeanor and avid adaptability to his surroundings, the young Leonard was finally adopted by a wealthy family from one of the more prestigious neighborhoods in Washington. After spending a considerable amount of time in several modest, yet respectable orphanages, he had finally gotten the break of his life. However, those feelings of not being good enough never left him. This was obviously the reason why he tried so hard in everything. Whether it was an illustrious education at private schools as a child, or a quick adaptability to higher education at Georgetown University, Caprese was always one to try harder. After graduating with honors, he chose to pursue politics. It was in this profession that he first got a taste of what power means. And it's an obsession that has never left him, burning like a furnace, deep within his soul. *I like being able to control my environment, he thought. And the puppets around me.*

Caprese and his colleagues—the Lieutenant, the bodyguard and Asghar's female bodyguard, were all Caprese's guests now. He wasn't sure how he had acquired Asghar's bodyguard, but she would serve him well, given that he lost both of his guards in the recent attack at this Nicaraguan estate. *Nothing like having an extremely beautiful killing machine at my side, Caprese mused to himself.*

It hadn't been a full 24 hours yet and he was already questioning his decision to take the hostages with him versus letting the pilot pick him up, while leaving the others behind—dead or alive. But it was too late. His decision had been made and now he would use it for his highest and best use.

Orchestrating an alternate plan was not difficult at all, given his third home here—safe from the wandering eyes of the governmental public. The beauty of holding a position of power in America gave him immense latitude when negotiating goods and services outside "The 50."

Caprese felt rather proud of himself for capturing the infamous Lieutenant Colonel Randall Matheson and "Boy

Wonder," Mr. Black—someone who he had learned was one of the top Navy Seals Ops, back in the day. The only way things could have been better would be if he'd also been able to snare Carter Matheson. Then again, if Caprese knew anything about the former Special Ops hit man known to those inside "The Bureau" as Lucky, it was that it wouldn't be long before their paths would cross again.

Caprese watched both Matheson and Black struggle to break free from the zip ties that anchored them to their chairs. The gags in their mouths were simply to keep them quiet, while transporting them to this secluded location. No need to attract any unnecessary attention. Caprese watched his sidekick remove the gags because they were clearly safe from wandering ears. As for his new bodyguard—emphasis on body, Caprese was going to find great pleasure in training her to his way of thinking.

"Just how stupid are you, Caprese?" barked Lt. Colonel Matheson, the moment the gag was removed.

Caprese said nothing and just smiled, fondling the ever-present cufflinks that adorned his expensive shirt.

Mr. Black turned his cold blue eyes from Caprese to Matheson, saying, "I'd say pretty fuckin' stupid. Two suits from top of the corp and..." He stopped, considering that Caprese didn't know Jennifer was Black's daughter. "A woman civilian. Yep, pretty stupid, LT," Black said to Randall, returning an icy stare to his captor.

Caprese nodded for his assistant and helicopter pilot, Jackson, to release the zip ties from the wrists and ankles of Xeon, motioning to have her join him in the chair next to him.

The privately managed hangar they were in was at the

opposite end of the property of the Jaime Gonzalez Airport terminal, just southeast of Cienfuegos, about 250 kilometers from Havana. It was far away from busy congestion—with the only real traffic from incoming planes. Most arriving planes approached from the Southeast, and this provided additional noise barriers for any unforeseen sounds that may come from the clandestine hangar. Cienfuegos is dubbed La Perla del Sur, or Pearl of the South, and provides the chief crops of sugarcane and coffee.

Caprese owned it along with two other men. One was a drug dealer with whom he had a quiet understanding—to stay out of one another's way, speak nothing of their respective proclivities and they would get along just fine. The other owner was a freelance pilot who ran helicopter tours for tourists, land developers and any other entrepreneurs who had a need for short hops to either the Cayman Islands, due south of them, or Key West, Florida, just north of them. Caprese and his small entourage used Cuba for yet another place of exile—far from suspecting politicos, ex or current girlfriends, or anyone who may be chasing him—as was likely the case, even now.

Jackson sat Xeon in the chair next to Caprese then stood behind both of them, awaiting orders. Matheson and Black looked at one another, keeping their game faces on, but wondering what was going to happen next.

"Not to worry, gentlemen," Caprese grinned, reading their minds. "I'm not going to hurt your little beauty. Quite the contrary. I'm going to treat her with the utmost of care. After all, she's about to become the latest soldier in my personal war."

Xeon didn't show any fear. Instead, she played up to

Caprese, posturing herself away from her team and all but batting her eyelashes at her new boss. Xeon knew that she would be in a much stronger, although more dangerous situation, if she stayed close to Caprese. That was, after all, her plan all along. Now, it all just became easier.

4.

THE DISCOVERY

SUNDAY, MAY 2 — 1111Z

I arrive at Miami International Airport and grab a shuttle to Landmark Aviation—a private hangar at the corner of 36th Street and 57th Avenue. On the opposite side of the main terminal, it housed primarily private corporate jets, personally owned helicopters and—unknown to most civilians, was the base to a very select group of current and former military brass who enjoyed meeting each month. Here they would talk sports, compare golf scores and discuss their weapons of choice. It was a Members Only Club without official rules or monthly dues. After all, members played by their own rules and had long ago paid their dues.

Arriving in just under three hours, I calculated that I'd beat Mack by about twenty minutes, so I nodded a hello to the front desk manager and took a seat in the far corner to wait. The view of the airfield would provide me a point of distraction, while I ran a series of potential scenarios.

A waitress named Tiffany approaches and asks if I'd like anything. I order a black coffee and a plate of fries.

"Mayo on the side, right?" she asks, flirting with her eyes.

"You remembered."

My phone interrupted our friendly banter with a text message: Just landed. Grabbing transpo to hangar. See you shortly. She walked away and I smiled, appreciating both her long legs and Mack's punctuality.

If I were Caprese, where would I be headed? My mind raced back to the memo from headquarters. It said they would have left shortly after 01:00, which means they'd arrive in Miami sometime around 04:00. That shouldn't be too tough, I'll just check...

I glanced up to see Mack coming through the door—his arm around the waitress. Both were laughing about something. I stood to greet them, shaking Mack's hand.

"Hey bro, Tiffany and I were just talking."

I took his bag and put it next to mine. "Yeah? About what?"

"She said that it was her birthday, day before yesterday." He raised his eyebrows. "And was telling me that she and a few friends had just flown in from the Cayman Islands. Seem's they were hanging out here having a few, when Tiffany overheard the name Caprese mentioned by a few men she hadn't seen here before."

His expression told me to engage.

"Really?" I said—continuing my flirtations from earlier, but turning them down a notch. "He was here?"

She nodded and my mind switched channels. Cayman Islands...of course, I thought. That would be a perfect hiding place.

She looked around then lowered her voice, "You know we're not supposed to talk—too loudly—about who was where or when," she grinned, "But you guys are regulars, so I thought maybe I could help. Mack tells me you had a run in with this fellow Caprese, but that you...lost him?"

I motioned for both of them to come closer. I knew Tiffany from flights in and out of Miami, and while we were only acquaintances, I was pretty sure she could be trusted. Mack took a seat and Tiffany leaned over the table. Checking her watch, she mumbled, "I'm off in less than twenty, so what the heck."

I pulled out a chair.

"Thanks."

"Let's just say we had a meeting with him," I said. "But this Caprese left...unexpectedly. He was supposed to come with us, but had some friends...who had other plans."

I looked around for eavesdropping ears. There were only six other people in the lounge, besides us. Four were in deep conversation, while the other two had their eyes glued to the TV screen over the bar.

"Bro? The girl's legit," Mack said, nodding to Tiffany to explain.

Tiffany pulled a shield from her pocket. It was a private detective's badge.

"What?"

She cut me a look that said, Dumbass.

"Okay. I just never..."

"Can you say, cover?"

"Copy that," I said, smiling at her then shaking my head to Mack.

"See?" he said.

"Anyway..." I reply.

"Anyway, we were coming back from the Caymans. Like Mack said, it was my birthday. Took some time off for scuba-diving with some friends. But it was time to get back. It was late, we had private access—like most of these clients," Tiffany said, nodding to the rest of the room. "So, as we're heading in, I overheard that name. Then, I remembered his showing up here and overheard him saying something about being on his way to his ranch somewhere outside..."

"Nicaragua?" I interrupt.

"That's it." She nods, hesitating a moment before adding, "I'd always wondered why someone with that...position...would hang out here, but we all know it's all about connections."

"Pun intended?" I smiled.

"Exactly." She volleyed. "And who we know...not necessarily what."

Smart girl, I thought, And what better place to play waitress than in a room full of players.

"So?" I say.

"That's all I really know," she replies. "Me and friends. In the Caymans. His name. Coincidence? Perhaps."

Mack and I looked at one another and shook our heads simultaneously. I wasn't sure what to think. And the hesitation said the same.

"Well, gents, it was nice, but I'm outta here. Got biz to catch up on. And frankly...that's all I got."

We stood. "No, that's great. Thanks. Anything is a help. As you can imagine, we're very interested in finding him..."

"And his friends," she interrupts.

"And his friends. And, as soon as we can."

"Thanks, Tiffany. You're swell," Mack adds.

"Ta-Ta for now," she says, turning to leave.

We both watch her exit and sit back down.

"Well, as cute as she is…"

"Got that right," Mack chimes in.

"And as helpful as that was…"

"It could be," he added.

"We're not really that much closer—as I'd already considered The Caymans…"

"Ditto."

"Imagine that. On the same page, yet that page may not be the exact page we need."

"True."

I finished my coffee, we both grabbed a couple of fries. Checking my watch, I slowly say, "Do you suppose we should be getting…"

John, from the front desk, approached us. "Your pilot will be ready in less than ten. He's just finishing a fuel up and equip check, and you'll be good to go."

"Thanks," I said, as he handed us some papers then left. "Shall we?" I added, nodding toward the tarmac.

"Why not?" Mack asks.

Heading toward the exit, my eyes scan the room. I look at the faces.

Nothing.

I check the television screens. Who cares?

It's then that my eyes land on a map on the far wall. For some reason it gets my attention. I smack Mack's arm and nod for him to join me.

"What's up?"

"I don't know," I absently reply, looking at the map of the coast of Miami…Key West…the Bahamas…and the Cayman Islands. I look at the triangle it makes. I study the distance between Nicaragua...and Costa Rica...then the Cayman Islands.

"You think he's sitting in the Caymans?" Mack asks.

"Could be. But why?"

"It's so small, we'd find him pretty quick," he says.

I nod.

Scanning the map, I try to figure out the play.

"C'mon, you're Lucky, for crap sake. I know you've got an idea percolating in that noggin' of yours. Just spit it out."

"Uh huh."

We stare a few moments longer. Nothing's popping.

"We've got a few minutes." I finally say. My eyes go from my watch to the private jet a hundred yards away. "He could have hopped over to the Cayman Islands. If so, he'd be there in, what, a buck-forty?"

"Yeah, less than two hours," Mack agrees, staring intently at the map.

"If he made it here," I say, pointing to the map, "It'd take him another hour and change. Let's call it three hours...to here," I point.

"Copy that."

"That certainly makes sense. He'd return, amidst all this, and disappear into the crowd."

I stop to see how that feels.

"Then he'd bounce up to DC on a connector."

I stop again. "Wait a second. Follow me," I say, motioning for him to join me at the front desk.

"Hey John, Mack and I are in Miami on...well, official business and we were wondering..."

Reaching for a clipboard, he starts scanning flight traffic logs. He looks at us, hesitates, then says, "You didn't get this from me—even if you are on official business." John barely cracks a smile. "What do you need? And, which day?"

Mack answers, "Two days ago. Let's check after 01:00 to, say, today. Any Bell 429's coming in around that time?"

John scans another set of pages, flips one, then another and shakes his head. "Not here. 'Course, there's two of these on the property. But then this is the one..."

"Right," I said, knowing that he means this location is the go-to HQ for Officers, Politicians, the Money-crowd, etcetera. "But..." I hesitate. "Nothing?"

"Nope."

"Wait a minute," I mumble. "A Bell 429 holds...what, 300 gallons?" I ask John, but turn to Mack to confirm.

"That's about right," Mack answers.

John responds, "256. US; to be exact. That's 217 in the main and 39 in the aux."

I calculate in my head, "Okay, so Liberia, Costa Rica—our liftoff point, to here is about what, a thousand miles?"

"1104. Point 91. Call it eleven-hundred miles," John adds, checking a chart taped to his side of the counter, between he and I.

I begin again to do the math, while John pulls out a calculator.

"Okay, 256 divided by..." I start.

"138.2 miles."

"Bingo!" I reply, snapping my fingers.

"They couldn't have made it—in perfect conditions, from DOQ to MIA." Mack answers.

John shakes his head just as I'm saying, "Nope."

I tap Mack on the shoulder and start back toward the map, but stop, spin around and add, "John, thank you. You have no idea how that helps."

"Sure enough. And your jet's up," he says, adding, "Pilot's at the ready."

I give him a signed waiver and nod for Mack to join me back at the map.

"Guess what, buddy?" I ask Mack.

"What's that?"

Once at the map, I slide my finger from DOQ to Miami, "This path? No go." I slide my finger from DOQ to Cayman Islands. "This? No go."

"What?"

"Hold on."

Then I slide my finger from DOQ to the island—rather, the country that lies in between. "Here."

"Cuba."

"Holy shit," he says, knowing my hunch is spot on.

"Damn skippy."

5.

THE RETRIEVAL

SUNDAY, MAY 2 — 1157Z

Caprese stood across the hangar talking quietly on his cellphone. Matheson and Black stared straight ahead, calculating their next move and knowing what each was likely thinking. Military partners had an unusual sixth sense about one another, especially in situations as heightened and dangerous as this. With stoic faces, they had a pretty good idea what was going to happen next. They would be either held for ransom—which wasn't likely; Caprese had all the money he needed and despised the intrinsic hassle. The other possible scenario was the more painful of the two: death. This was more likely. They were both certain they'd be used as pawns for some negotiation or another. The fact wasn't lost on Randall that he had not only orchestrated the takeover of Caprese—in his own home, but also humiliated him in front of business colleagues. The one alliance, Asghar

Debashi, would have given him the exact tool he needed to more deeply entrench him into a place he so desperately wanted. That strategic alliance would have given him the key to his future and ultimate position of power in the White House. The most important thing that Caprese needed now was exile. And he had that in this country.

Jackson rechecked his rifle. Part of his ruse was to appear disinterested, or distracted. But he wasn't. He watched his boss on the phone—always talking business. He eyeballed Matheson and Black, wondering what they were planning—knowing whatever it was, he'd be one step ahead of them. He also closely watched Xeon, trying to ascertain something between her and the two men. There seemed to be some sort of bond. It was nearly imperceptible. What was Jackson sensing? He knew from doing his research that she was the bodyguard of Asghar Debashi. But what was chewing at him? He thought about mentioning something to Caprese, but knew well enough that Caprese would have picked up on it some time ago. On the other hand, if he didn't say anything and things happened differently later, there would be hell to pay. Checking his watch, he noted that enough hours had passed since their arrival and that they had a healthy head-start on Carter and his crew. He'd let it rest. For now.

Hanging up the phone, Caprese took his time walking across the hangar to join his captives. What I want more than anything is to have Carter in my sights, he thought. That fact alone would not only satisfy his competitive lust—knowing that he was the superior brain at work, but would also let him rest easy knowing that once he got rid of Carter, he would never again have to look over his shoulder. Given that he held Carter's father captive guaranteed his impending arrival. If Caprese knew anything about Carter's methodology and drive, it was that he was certain, beyond a shadow of doubt, Carter would arrive sooner rather than later—likely inside the next 24 to 48 hours. That was the rule: find subjects in under 48, or dramatically increase the likelihood of never finding them. I've got to secure my fortress and prepare, he thought. What works to my favor is that Carter thinks I'm back in Miami.

Caprese looked at Xeon, as he approached the trio. He was happy to be adding this new ally to his command. She had the training, the heart, the strength and, as an added bonus, the looks. Perhaps she only needed the extra touch he provided, thus making the two of them unstoppable. Hell, this could be love, he thought. Never. That just complicates everything.

"Gentlemen, I'm so happy to have a new partner in crime join me. She's so much easier on the eyes than my former team, don't you think?"

"I don't give a hot, steaming shit what you're planning to do with your new little girlfriend here, Caprese!" Randall barked. "All I care is that you use that dull globe of yours and think for a minute. You plan on doing anything stupid with me and my pal here? There's going to be a shit-storm that'll rain down on your head so bad…and so deep…you won't know which end is up."

Matheson was covering a bit of his bravado with bluff. He didn't know where he was because as soon as he and the other two boarded their helicopter in Liberia, their hands were bound, as they were gagged then drugged. They were headed for San Jose, where they would jump a private Lear to Miami. However, instead they got intercepted by

Caprese and his team. All of these facts were slowly coming back to him, as the sleeping agent wore off. Randall may be sluggish, but he wasn't scared, because he had been in tighter places before.

"You miserable littler twerp—thinking you can simply kidnap the three of us, keep us stowed away in who knows where and expect us to just sit and take it," Randall added, knowing that was punching Caprese's buttons. Randall could feel Caprese getting angry and he enjoyed it.

The corners of Caprese's mouth slowly dropped, turning a semi-pleasant smile into a stone-cold face. His nostrils flared and his eyes squinted. But Caprese wasn't going to show his anger.

Don't let them see you feel, Caprese thought, walking around the men, both strapped into chairs. He stepped closer, getting within inches of Randall's face.

"Not that you have much of a choice, now do you, Lieutenant?" Caprese said, wiping his brow of sweat. It was getting hot fast and the heat inside this hangar would steadily climb for the rest of the day.

"That's some big talk coming from a big man...who has gotten himself into a big mess. Because from where I stand...it looks as though you have no bargaining power. None at all, actually." You arrogant fat man, Caprese thought.

"Really?" Randall nodded. "Well, considering that I was enlisted and preparing to fight for my country, while you were still shitting your diapers...and I have the mental acuity that far surpasses yours...I'd say I'm just fine." Randall let that hang in the air before pushing his captor one step further.

"We may be incapacitated—for now, but at least we're not

incapable of carrying out a mission."

They stared at each other—waiting for what was next. Neither of them flinched.

"Your arrogance is incomprehensible. You may have found my little getaway in Nicaragua...you may have gotten the inside word on my business dealings with Debashi, but frankly, you know so very little as to my big picture. And right now? I hold the cards."

"You're insane, Caprese," Mr. Black said, speaking directly to him for the first time since they arrived. "Certifiably insane."

Caprese looked at Black with no expression. "I may be insane, as you put it, but I'm only insane for thinking that our current President has any idea what he's doing in office...besides being more preoccupied with his social media status than running this country with an iron fist. He's the most inept President in the history of our country."

The room gets quiet.

"Is that what this is about?" Randall asked, putting the pieces together, "You have a grudge against the President? Do you...are you vying for his job?" Randall started laughing. That made Black chuckle, and before long, Randall and Black were laughing uncontrollably.

Caprese was furious. He walked over to Jackson, pointing at the 9mm in his holster. Jackson removed and handed it to Caprese. He walked over to Randall and Black, loaded the chamber and pointed it at Randall's forehead. That stopped his laughing. He then pointed the gun at Black and shot him in the foot.

BANG!

Black screamed. "What the fuck!"

He desperately wanted to grab his foot, but couldn't, so Black fought the urge to come unglued and instead took several long, deep breaths—lowering his heart rate and calming his adrenaline. Within minutes, it was as though nothing happened; however, there was a small pool of blood just beneath his foot.

Randall fought to get out of his chair, and shouted at Caprese, "You stupid prick. You got a beef—shoot ME!"

Caprese considered it—but just for a moment. He needed Randall in order to get to Carter.

Remember that, Caprese thinks.

Xeon wanted to jump from her chair and onto the back of Caprese and choke him within an inch of his life. Instead, she looked at Jackson, gave him a wicked smile, then coldly said to Caprese, "Nice work, Dr. Caprese."

This was just enough to stop the momentum and Caprese lowered the gun, took a deep breath and smiled at Xeon.

"Shut up, Xeon," Randall barked, "And enough dick swinging, Caprese. Just tell us what you want and let's get on with it."

Returning the gun to Jackson and his attention to Randall, he continued, "I'm growing impatient and…" he looked at his Cartier, "Time is growing short." He motioned for Jackson to join him as he headed for the door. "Besides, I've much more important things to do."

6.

THE COMPETITION

SUNDAY, MAY 2 — 1258Z

Outside the building, about two-hundred yards away from the entrance to the hangar doors, stood a group of hard-looking men carrying automatic rifles. They numbered about a dozen.

One of Caprese's hangar-mates is Donovan Blair. Known among his peers as Scorpion, Donovan is an extremely large, yet handsomely rugged man with piercing blue eyes. He and Caprese met several years ago and have a simple and quiet agreement to handle business in a professional manner. Or else. Their paths rarely crossed, but when they did, it seemed to teeter on a volatile blend of testosterone and danger, with a dash of mutual admiration. Wearing black from head to toe, Donovan has a gun holstered in his belt and slung low for easy retrieval. A large knife is strapped to his other leg and an Uzi slung over his shoulder completing the hardware arsenal. He looked like he's ready to go to combat; however, in every occasion or photograph in which Caprese has seen him, he looked the same way—even walking down the street. He is a man to be feared and not taken lightly.

As Caprese and Jackson exited, Jackson held the door for Caprese and was about to follow when Caprese stopped him. Taking his time, Caprese scanned the tarmac then turned his full attention to Jackson.

"Wait inside with them."

"But—"

"But nothing. It's more important to keep an eye on them than to join me."

Jackson shifted his focus from Caprese's cold eyes to the shielded eyes of the men across the tarmac. He thought, I don't want to miss anything, but realized his boss made the call. Period.

"It's Carter we're after. And the only way we're going to get him in our grip...again...is for us to securely hold the one thing that's most important to him." Caprese nods toward inside.

"Copy that," Jackson said quietly, not taking his eyes off the men. "What about them?"

Caprese thought, Are you joking? Like you could do anything to them, then said, "They're not your concern." And with that, his focus went from Jackson to the men across the concrete.

Jackson began to walk away, when Caprese spoke.

"Do I need to explain what having Carter in our control means?"

"No, Sir. You don't."

Caprese replied with a quiet "Good" and started walking toward his colleagues.

Donovan's eyes dart from one man to the next. He locked eyes, punctuating sentences with short nods that further conveyed his seriousness. He didn't like, nor did he ever, repeat himself.

Eleven peers, including him, make a dirty dozen; twelve of the most feared men in all of Cuba and the neighboring islands. They are known for lethal and stealth procedures of illicit drug procurement and distribution. And while all of the men are wanted on multiple counts, none of them except Donovan, have ever done time. But he got caught on purpose, for the mere connections he could make inside the system—both behind and in front of the bars.

The Scorpion always has a singular if not stinging purpose in everything he does. It's that focused intent that makes him millions of dollars a year, makes dozens of allies a month, and makes many dead, along the way.

"Okay, so our next intercept is at 18:00. We've got a team coming up from Honduras and another from Jamaica. They should arrive about the same time. Needless to say, I need all hands on deck. And don't forget..." He stopped just as he sensed Caprese getting within earshot.

He turned and stared at Caprese, expressionless. If it weren't for the fact Donovan had a healthy respect for Caprese, one of his men would have cut him down with a single shot without blinking an eye.

"Donovan," Caprese nodded.

"Caprese. What's on your mind?" he replied, adding, "Like I don't already have some sort of an idea what your sick mind is up to." He cracked a rare and nearly imperceptible grin. His perfect white teeth shined in the hot morning sun.

"I have something, or rather, someone that may be of interest to you. He's inside—along with his trusty companion."

"Okay." He hesitated. "And how does that interest me?"

Caprese finally acknowledged the men that surrounded him. He knew whatever he wanted to share, it's safe to do so in front of them. This group was inseparable.

"Let's just say that with their legal approval of inbound shipments…your job could become easier."

This had Donovan's attention.

Squinting, he clenched his jaw and scanned the eyes of his men. He barked to his group, "Fall out and meet upstairs in…" He checked his watch, "In 30. Champ and Sparks, you run the schedule one more time. Birdman, Parrot, gas and pack the Helo. Gorilla, Blade, you come with me. The rest of you relax. We've got time."

The men scattered without a word, while Gorilla, Scorpions bodyguard—not that he appeared to need one, and Blade, the groups weapons specialist, flanked Donovan. They fell into step with Caprese who was already making his way toward the hangar.

"So, who are these men?" Donovan asked. "And with my group, what makes you think I need any help?"

"Like I implied; you don't need them, as much as you may be able to use them to expedite things. I'm holding them for entirely different reasons."

Donovan grunted, "That sounds clandestine."

Caprese chuckled. "You could say that."

7.

THE CHASE

SUNDAY, MAY 2 — 1259Z

Mack and I jump aboard the company's Lear 45XR and are on our way. With a nautical speed of Mach .81, or roughly 620 MPH, we were on course to make it from Miami to Havana in under an hour.

I was short on patience, but it wouldn't be long before the two of us would be reunited with that idiot Caprese. What he's up to is anyone's business, I ponder. We barely returned to our normal when this jackass disrupts our lives, once again.

"What's eating you, boss?" Mack asks, in between bites of a Cliff bar. I could tell he was wound tight; that was the second one he'd eaten in the last 15 minutes.

"Just thinking," I grunt. "Trying to figure out this clown's play."

Stretched out and taking up two seats, Mack's size was intimidating. But nothing was as unnerving as his stare.

And he had just a bit of that wicked look right now, aiming it straight at his best pal. I knew what he was thinking before he said it.

“We got him before. We’ll get him again. Prick.”

Leave it to Mack to put things succinctly. It was one of the things I admire about him. That and his ability to crush a man’s skull with his bare hands. I’d seen him do it in Iraq—when we were in a situation where silence was of utmost importance. He could have snapped his neck, or choked the man, except that the perp’s face was buried in the dirt, and all Mack wanted to do was to shut him up and not give away our position. Instead, just as the man struggled free and was about to scream, Mack crushed his skull. It was unnerving.

We rode in silence for a few minutes before I theorized what Caprese may be up to.

“Suppose he’s thinking something along the line of a ransom,” I said.

“I’m thinking the same.”

“That’s what I…It wasn’t a question; it was a statement.”

“Right,” Mack says.

“Obvious, I know.” I shake my head. “It’s not like we need a Dick Tracy Detective Kit to figure that out. It’s just what he wants—that’s what’s got me simmering. Why LT, Black and Xeon?”

Mack nods. “Collateral.”

“Yeah. He’s got plenty of money. Much, if not all of it has to be hidden in oversea accounts. He must have lots of property…”

“Minus one property,” Mack interjects, chuckling.

“True. That spread in Nicaragua was something else.”

“I’ll miss that boat.”

"So will Steph," I say, hesitating to think about my girl. "Like I was saying, you know he's got any number of places spread all over the world. And he'll have one in Havana, too. IF indeed that's where he's set up."

Mack stretches and says, "What makes you think Havana?"

I start to speak when I realize I don't have a fast answer. "Good question," I say, staring out the window to the wide open blue.

"Right?"

"Right," I reply. "It's just an assumption. And a good place to start."

"True."

The pilot opens the cabin door. "We'll land in less than 20, guys."

We both nod. He gives a thumbs up and closes the door. We look at one another but say nothing.

"What if..." I start. "Do you suppose..." I add, quickly reaching to my duffle bag to get a map I confiscated from the clubhouse at the Miami hangar. "Let's take a look."

Mack brushes the crumbs off his shirt and eyeballs the map I've spread across an empty seat. He rubs his hands together as if they were ice cold. It's his sign for I'm excited—let's do this.

"El Ramon would be a likely point to the East. And Santiago de Cuba, to the South" I say, scanning my finger along the paper, searching for an impulse from my intuition.

"What about all the way West, like Sandino?" Mack asks.

"Maybe. But somehow I doubt he'd be that far. No likely place to land and store." I think for another few moments then add, "Maybe Southwest, like Manzanillo."

"How about going solo?" Mack says.

"Huh?"

"How about Nueva Gerona?" He taps the map. "Pretty fucking remote, huh?"

"Yeah, maybe too remote. There needs to be some action around. To blend in. Disappear among the crowds."

"Agreed."

"My money's on Trinidad." I point to the area. "Look. Just off the coast. Near some jungle—if need be. Access to..." I hesitate. "Santa Maria? Maybe that airport's too far."

"But maybe it's a good place to start. That is IF Havana isn't the spot," Mack chimes in.

I nod, check my watch and decide we have to pick a stopping off point if Havana isn't our destination of choice. I fold the map and shove it back into my bag. Looking out the window, we're quickly approaching José Martí International Airport. It's seconds before we land.

Something doesn't feel right and I don't know why. Looking at Mack, I frown and pull the map out again and look.

"Doesn't feel right, does it?" he asks.

I shake my head, knowing something's off.

Making our final approach, the plane quickly descends.

Scanning the map, I look at other options. Water access. Nearby mountains. Downtown airport. What is it, dammit?

We eyeball one another, searching for anything that feels right.

Just as the pilot lights up the seatbelt sign, pinging the accompanying bell, Mack and I, right on cue simultaneously say, "Cienfuegos."

After a very abrupt, last-minute detour, the pilot rapidly

climbed several thousand feet in a matter of seconds and redirected us, landing just a few minutes further south. Within minutes, we arrive José Martí International Airport and are in a borrowed car heading to the center of town. I didn't want to lose another minute without starting our search. The clock was ticking and we had no idea what Caprese was planning. For all we knew, Caprese had our boys for the pleasure of playing with me. Worse, he could be torturing them as payback for our dropping his two companions in the ground in Nicaragua. Doubtful. One thing I was pretty sure of: Caprese wouldn't have a soft spot for anyone if his life depended on it. Hell, he'd sell his own family for a chance to run the country, I thought to myself, while scanning the horizon for anything to ping my radar.

We pull up to a bodega and get out for a couple of espressos. We wanted to blend in for now and just size the place up.

"Yo, Lucky, see the '55 Bel Air at 10 o'clock?" Mack says quietly, looking in the opposite direction.

I scan to my left, keeping my head turning well past the spot he was referring to; my Raybans helped keep my surveillance intact.

"Copy."

There were two men in the front seat and another one standing outside the car smoking a cigarette. All eyes were locked on me and Mack.

"Could be coincidence."

"Don't believe in coincidences," I reply, sipping my espresso while looking for any other cars and/or men in the area that were paying as much attention to us as these three.

"See that tour stand just to the right of them?" Mack asks, not waiting for a reply, "I'll head that way. You see what they do."

"Copy that." I hand the vendor another couple of bucks and engage in some mindless conversation, while watching Mack make his way across the busy intersection. The driver and the smoker were both watching him, but the passenger's gaze constantly shifted from me to something in his lap, and back.

Mack is nearly at the stand when the smoker gets in the back seat and leans forward to say something. Mack takes a tourist map from the tour stand, handing a vendor some change and looks at it then to me. I tap my chest, referencing the camera he'd strapped around his neck and he lifted it to take some pictures. Just then, the car pulls away. He swings in their direction and snaps off several shots of their license plate. I nod for him to head back, we jump in the car and follow them.

8.

THE RENDEZVOUS

SUNDAY, MAY 2 — 1421Z

Donovan and Caprese were still chatting in the corner of the hangar—one eye, on the captives, and the other on a notebook Caprese shared with Donovan. Jackson sat motionless in a chair a few dozen feet from where his captives sat. Black's head was drooping and the pool of blood under his foot had grown. Randall was worried; the shifting look between Black and his daughter showed his concern. Jackson wasn't. He didn't care one way or the other. As far as he was concerned, they were just extra baggage weighing the whole process down.

Tony Black had endured a good deal of pain in his day, so this was nothing new. The biggest problem was that his hands were handcuffed behind his back and his arms were bound to the chair with a rope. This allowed him no room to maneuver. On top of that difficulty, blood continued to slowly seep from his foot, while his blood pressure slowly dropped. The sweat on his brow and pale color made it obvious he was approaching a dangerous place.

Xeon sat silent, moving nothing but her eyes from the automatic rifle Jackson had laying across his lap, loosely pointed in the direction of Randall, to her father who was clearly starting to fade. He needed attention and she was going to get it.

"Dr. Caprese, can I have a word with you, please?" she cooed in his direction. Given she wasn't bound like the others and she was his new bodyguard, made for some interesting possibilities.

Caprese nodded and held up a single finger to suggest, Just a moment. She smiled in return and appeared in no hurry. As Jackson shifted his gaze between she and Caprese, he appeared a bit surprised as she smiled at him. She liked that she had just added some mystery to the equation. As he turned to look in the opposite direction, she loosened her blouse; this would certainly help distract Jackson a bit further, as her more than ample breasts got every man's attention. He turned to look and couldn't help but stare. And she liked it.

Caprese and Donovan joined the quartet in the middle of the room. The heat from the day, as well as the subconscious heat of the moment was clearly building, and it wouldn't be long before this kettle would begin to boil.

"Yes?" Caprese asked her.

"I'm going to get some water and a bandage for this guy," she said, confidently taking matters into her own hands. "Can you direct me to where that might be?"

Caprese grinned, admiring her take-charge attitude. Donovan, on the other hand, had never seen her before

and despite her beauty, wasn't sure she was to be trusted.
"Just a minute, little lady," Donovan said, holding his hands out and stopping her from crossing the room. "This is as much my place as his," he nodded toward Caprese, "And I'm not so sure you're...well...one of us."
She felt a cold tingle go up her spine. That wasn't good. Did he make me? She wondered, Or was he just showing off his sack? Either way, she didn't get to where she was in life without being bold.
"Not sure what you're getting at, Sir, but this little lady is going to help this guy out...just so he doesn't bleed out and die on our asses."
Donovan couldn't quite decide if he was pissed at her insubordination, or turned on by her kick-ass attitude. "You have some vested interest in this man?"
She wouldn't back down now.
"Me? Give a shit. Don't know who he is. But I work for Dr. Caprese now, and as much as he may be a dangerous man, he's not a stupid man. And my intuition tells me that he would want to draw as little attention to his life...and this place...as was possible. And if this man's ass dies on us, then someone—likely me, will have to dispose of his body."
"She has a good point, Donovan," Caprese added, smiling.
"Like I say, I don't even know him, but look at me," she held her hands out, highlighting her great figure, "Do you think I'm going to blend in while carrying some douche-bag wrapped up in an old, worn carpet?"
Donovan checked his watch. He's running behind.
"Whatever. Water? Yes. Bandages? We don't have any. Besides, he'll manage," he said, starting to leave. "I gotta bounce. My men are waiting for me. Do what you want,

Caprese. And while I appreciate your offer to let the Lieutenant Colonel's cred help me at the dock, I think I've got it handled. You carry on with your little ransom plan and I'll catch up with you later."

He was nearly toward the door when his cellphone beeped. He took it from his belt, checked the screen, spun around to look out the window and saw a car heading his way. He turned back to see Xeon walking toward the office and Jackson trying to decide whether to follow her or stay with Caprese.

"Jackson!" he shouted.

This startled the guard, who spun toward Donovan. A healthy fear was on his face.

"Yes?"

"Keep one eye and your gun on the soldier—the bodyguard..." He looked at Black and shook his head. "He won't give you much trouble. And keep your other eye on her." He was out the door before Jackson could respond.

Caprese turned to Jackson and added, "You heard the man."

If I didn't know better, the car that was following Mack and I was driving as if they wanted us to follow. We had followed them for nearly two dozen blocks—but, who's counting?

"Do you get the same feeling I do?" I ask.

"You mean like...why aren't they trying harder to ditch us?"

"Exactly."

"Funny. I was just thinking the same thing."

"Imagine that."

I back off, just to prove the point. In fact, I purposely hang a quick left down a side street, pull over to the curb and park for a minute. Mack and I look at one another.

“One-thousand-one…One-thousand-two…One-thousand-three…One-thousand-four…” I look in the rearview mirror. “Bingo.”

The car appears, a little too quickly for comfort and slows down.

Checking the side mirror, Mack says, “What the frack?”

The car drives by, but this time, there’s only one person in the car.

“Interesting,” I say, turning to Mack and suggesting we play along. “Shall we?”

“Of course. After you,” he says in his best Chip & Dale voice. I snort.

Picking up speed, I get right on his tail.

“Pull around and get in front,” Mack barks, pulling his .45 from its holster.

One swift move later and I’m right beside him. While I’m just short of pushing him to the curb, I get him to stop. The driver gets out in an instant, but Mack already beats him to the punch, pointing his .45 at his face.

“What the fuck, dude?” yells the perp—his accent sounding more Californian than Cuban. He barely has time to pull his gun from the holster.

I pull my Glock and point it directly at the corner of the street where we just came from, fully expecting his partners to round it any minute.

“What the fuck with you…dude? Mack yells, adding, “Drop the gun—before I drop you.”

The guy doesn’t budge.

Mack yells, “Now!”

The misfit slowly lays his gun on the roof of the car.

In the meantime, I don’t take my eyes off that street

corner.

"Where are they, hombre?" I ask.

"Don't know what you're talking about, bro."

"I'm not your fuckin' bro…and you're going to tell me why you're following us, why you pulled a gun on us and where the hell your compadres are," I shout, "Or else!"

Just then, his cellphone chirps. He doesn't budge.

"Answer it. Slowly. Or, I'll pop a hole in our chest so fast you'll be dark before you hit the dirt."

"Okay. Give it a rest, dude, I'm cool," he answers, slowly reaching for the phone and answering it. "Yep. Yep," he says, looking at Mack then back to me, adding, "Yes, they do."

Staring at me, he says, "Hold on," and hands me the phone.

I look at the screen, checking to see if it's a bomb. It reads: BOSS.

"Hello?"

"Carter?" the baritone voice says.

"Yeah."

"I see you met my friends."

"One of them. Who is this?"

There's a long beat before he says, "People know me as Scorpion. Friends call me Donovan. You can call me…shit storm about to rain on you."

"Yeah, well, we'll see about that," I confidently reply.

"I'd say I will see about that. And you may want to drop your gun. The same goes for your friend."

I knew something was up because the hair on the back of my neck stood up in a way I didn't like. I started to turn my head, when he continued.

"I wouldn't do that. I have two scopes zeroed in on both of

your heads."

"Uh huh."

"Uh huh is right, smart-ass. See the top floor balcony? There at the corner, where you turned not two minutes ago...trying to lose my men?"

I look. Sure enough, tucked behind a scrubby potted plant comes the flash of a red beam. I look down to see it wiggle back and forth in the dead center of my chest.

I grunt.

"Now, turn to see your partner. And tell him not to do anything stupid."

I turn to see Mack looking at me with a wrinkled brow.

"Hold tight, partner," I say, slowly looking around, "And don't move."

The voice in my ear continues, "Now, turn a little further. See that piece-o-shit van at the corner?"

I hear him say something in a muffled voice.

"The faded black one? I see it."

The window lowers, exposing a high-powered rifle—just like the one I use for Special Ops.

"It's pointed directly at the back of your buddies head. One move and all you'll see is a red mist."

I see the red dot wiggle again—this time, it's on the back of Mack's skull.

"Copy that," I say, trying to make spit in my dry mouth. "So, what's next?"

"Two things. Pretty simple. Get one wrong? You're dead. Get them both wrong, and you're both dead."

"I'm listening."

"Good. First: slowly hand your gun to my friend there. You can call him Pony, just to be polite."

I want to make a fast move, but given my chest could be

spaghetti in the blink of an eye, I don't. Instead, I say, "Here...Pony."

"What the fuck's going on, Carter?" Mack barks, starting to walk toward me.

"STOP!" I yell, whipping my head in his direction. "Don't move, Mack. Trust me."

"Excellent. I see you're playing ball with me," Scorpion calmly says in my ear. "Now. For number two: Tell him to lay his gun on the roof of the car and place both hands on the top of his head. And be sure he interlocks his fingers. Then wait, or, he'll be sorry."

"Mack. Lay your piece on the hood. Step back. Put your hands on the top of your head. And lock your fingers."

"Fuck that!"

"Uh, no. Let's just play along, okay?" I look him dead in the eye. "Trust me, these guys are in control," I add, flicking my eyes left and adding a tiny nod. I then look down and slowly turn—just enough for him to see the red laser wiggling on my chest.

"Copy that," he calmly says, laying down the gun and grabbing the top of his head.

"Good work," the voice says, "Now, give us 60 seconds and we'll all be on our way."

"Where to?" I ask.

"You'll know soon enough. But trust me, you'll like it. That is, if you want to see your father again. Alive."

9.

THE REUNION

SUNDAY, MAY 2 — 1522Z

We arrived at the Jaime Gonzalez Airport in less than 20 minutes. Scorpion's men didn't waste any time zip-tying and tossing us in the back of the van I'd spotted in our showdown on the side street. I wasn't sure where Donovan was, or where he was positioned during that capture, but I'm certain we'd be meeting him face to face any minute now.

These were not the run-of-the-mill drug-runners; they were soldiers. I could tell by the artillery hidden inside the nondescript van. And I could decipher by the way they moved. Everything happened with perfect precision. No wasted motions. They had a method—a protocol. It was easy to see they meshed tightly, worked closely, and moved efficiently. They also didn't talk much; instead, kept their communication vague—no doubt, to keep wandering ears from piecing anything together.

At least my hunch as to what city the group was holed up in was correct, I thought, it could have taken us days, maybe weeks, to have located everyone. And while not happy being handcuffed and in the back of a nasty van with a couple of sweaty soldiers, I was glad to be on the right trail. One thing was for sure, Mack and I were going to get out of this in one piece. We'd been in much worse fixes before and it was just a matter of a few details and a few toys—most of which were inside wheel-wells of that car we left behind, or in a locker back at the airport. Those tools, along with a few maneuvers, would all come together shortly, if I have my way.

There we were: Mack and me, Black and LT, and Xeon makes five. Only thing was: the four of us were handcuffed, and the one of her was free and clear to maneuver. What the hell? I thought, but knew the answer in about 2 minutes. I scanned the room. It was full of men. I scanned Xeon. Her blouse was full of cleavage. Watching her work the pack of horn-dogs was a site to behold. I counted eleven men.

Geez, they've got a whole brigade. What's up? I think. At least Randall was alive and safe. Our eyes met and we shared a look that only a father and son would understand. His look said, You're okay. He smiled and nodded. I did the same.

He then cut his eyes toward Tony Black. His color was pale and from the pool of blood on the floor, it was obvious he wasn't doing so well.

Who would shoot a man in the foot, for crap sake? I thought.

I looked at Randall. He nodded toward Black's foot and frowned, then shook his head as if to say Can you believe it. His eyes went to Caprese.

Caprese and the man I assumed was Donovan were standing in the corner talking quietly. I had a pretty good idea where this was going. Or, at the very least, had an idea what the potential outcome could be—especially if our training over the past dozen years had amounted to much of anything. Caprese's cellphone rang. He motioned to his friend to give him a minute and walked across the room.

With eyes back on the eleven, I noticed they all had the appearance of soldiers. Every one of them. It wasn't necessarily their clothing, which was head-to-toe black. It was the way they stood, reacted to any word of movement Donovan would make. He's an enormous Mo-Fo, I thought. Reminds me of Dwayne "The Rock" Johnson, but with blue eyes and long hair. This had to be the drug gang I'd read about. The ones who were ruthless killers. They were reported to move more drugs into Miami than any group in the world. But why hadn't they ever been caught? This did not look like those types. But then...what does that type look like?

Mack and I were sitting in the middle of the hangar. Our wrists and ankles were tied with ropes—the type used for mountain climbing. They'd done a pretty good job of immobilizing us. At least neither of us were gagged. It wouldn't have mattered because either nobody would hear us, or would have given a shit. Either way, we're not screamers—we're killers.

Caprese walked over to join the small crowd and was the first to speak.

"Well, well...if it isn't an old-fashioned reunion."

"Caprese," I said, nodding, trying to be cordial. I wasn't

sure if doing so would help my chances of survival, but it was certainly worth the try.

"Carter. How nice to see you again. Even if you are in a different...condition than before. Nicaragua was such a...misunderstanding. While some things didn't work so well; others happened just as they should. Tell me, how does it feel to be my captive?" He grinned.

"Huh? Sorry, I was nodding off—what with that long story of yours. But these?" I added, looking at the ropes that had me bound, "They're pretty comfortable, actually."

The smile on Caprese's face slowly faded, as if melting downward. The light in his eyes also faded, as if to say, I was trying to be nice, but now I won't.

It didn't matter. We weren't friends. Never would be friends. In fact, I would have killed him in Nicaragua, if the opportunity had shown itself. And even though I don't hate him, I hate everything he stands for. And when he kidnapped my father, across International lines, and endangered his life, my ex-girlfriend's life and now my best pal's life? Well, now all bets are off. And I would stop at nothing to see him fry.

As if reading my mind, Caprese said, "I know you're just wishing me dead, Carter. It's all over your face. I stole your father and his best friend. Now, I have you and your best friend. That must really hurt." He waited, either for affect, or to see what I had to say. I said nothing. I just stared. And steamed.

"Okay, well," he continued, clapping his hands like he was attending a children's birthday party, "We must move on toward our next goal. World domination!" He laughed like a crazy man, then stopped to see if I found the humor in it.

"You're insane, Caprese," was all I could muster.

"Fuckin' looney tunes, if you ask me, buddy," Mack chimes in.

"I third that...you nut biscuit," Randall barks from a gravelly voice.

Caprese was not amused.

"Rat turd," Black mumbles, without lifting his head.

All three of our heads whipped in his direction, as we thought he'd been passed out this whole time. He slowly lifts his head, looks at us, grins and resumes his nearly comatose position.

"Well, I'd say that makes it unanimous," Mack adds, "You fuck stick!"

You could tell by Caprese's slightly flared nostrils and slowly erecting posture that he was not happy. And he would most certainly do something about it. Thing was—we weren't scared.

"You men," he said, shaking his head back and forth like a disappointed father, "Just don't get it. You play heroics and bravado and all that...bullshit. But it's truly a shame. You know why?" He hesitated, waiting for one of us to answer. "Because we—the group of us..." he continued, spreading his arms wide to include all the men standing behind him, "Could share the spoils of our labor, becoming more rich and powerful beyond anything you've ever imagined in your poor...miserable...small-minded...lives."

"We don't want what you're selling, Caprese," I said

I notice Donovan whisper something to several of his men. Then, as he approaches us, his crew splits into two groups; a group of six head toward the exit, while another group of five surrounds us.

My stomach tightens, as I hear Mack sigh. This wasn't going to be good.
Donavan approaches and looks from one to the next, and then back to me. He leans down in order to get close. He is within inches of my face. So close, in fact, I can smell old coffee on his breath and cigar from his clothes.
"So...you're the infamous Carter," he said, relishing each word.
I didn't budge.
"I've heard so much about you," he says, taking his time to look me up and down. "Funny thing; you're not as large in person as I'd imagined." He tilted his head to one side. Crack. And then to the other. More cracks. It sounded like someone stepping on peanut shells.
"Bigger...isn't always...better," I reply.
This gets a grin.
"I suppose. At lease you're smart. I'll give you that," he says, standing back up and adjusting himself. "But I'm not sure if I can tell if you're tremendously brave...or just plain dumb."
"Guess time will tell."
"Hmm...you're just full of cliches, aren't you? I expected more. Eh, maybe that's just nervous energy. Either way, we've got work to do. And as much as I'd enjoy standing around swinging cocks with you Jarheads—I've got business to accomplish."
He checks his watch then looks to who appears to be his second in command and says, "In fact, we're about to take control of one of the largest shipments ever transported across international waters. This time tomorrow, we'll have enough money to buy you and your entire army—several times over."

"That's Marines," I say.

In unison, Mack LT, Black and I say, "Oorah!

"Yeah. Whatever," he chuckles, motioning for one of his men to join him and the other four to sequester us. They began untying the ropes that held us to the chairs, but left the zip-ties in place. One man took care of me, one for Mack, one for Randall and one for Black. Black couldn't stand because of his foot, so his guy picked him up and tossed him over his shoulder like a rag doll. Between that display of strength, and the fact that the guy who had untied me grabbed my arm—nearly snapping it off in the process, I could tell these guys were all exceptionally fit. Even Mack winced as his guy jerked his arms behind him. Mack cut me a look that said, Uh oh.

Donovan spoke something into the ear of the last guy who stood next to him. He looks at Xeon, who hadn't spoken a word the whole time. He motions her over. When no-neck said, "You come with me," Caprese spoke up.

"No. She stays with me."

Donovan throws him a stare. "I don't know her. She hasn't been vetted with us. She may have seen and heard too much already," Donovan sternly said.

"She's fine. She's my new bodyguard. Assistant, really."

Donovan frowns, walks, over and gets right in Caprese's face. "That's just it; she's your new bodyguard. Maybe your assistant. I doubt you know her affiliation. Not really."

"I do, it's just—"

"Save it. I didn't get here by being reckless."

"I have to disagree," Caprese tries one more time.

Donovan's look stops Caprese. "Not going to risk it."

I've come to learn rather quickly that while Caprese isn't a man to back down, he was certainly making the choice to do so now. Maybe that was just for this moment, but it was clear that between Donovan's size and apparent strength—not to mention his entourage of roughnecks, he would do all the talking for now.

Addressing Xeon, Caprese nodds in our direction and said, "Go with them. You'll be fine."

"That's good advice, young lady," Donovan said with a smirk. He couldn't help but take one last glimpse at her ample figure. She frowns with a look that says, You disgust me, but says nothing. His smirk dissolved into an expressionless face, as he added a nod for Caprese to join him then left through the front door. Taking a last look at Xeon, Caprese follows, while the rest of us stood there looking at one another, not knowing what would come next.

10.

THE SHIPMENT

SUNDAY, MAY 2 — 1623Z

The afternoon was like most: hot, humid, and full of transportation business. Peter Coen loved his job. He'd moved from DC to the Keys a dozen winters ago and never looked back. He hated the cold, the traffic and the bureaucracy. As the owner of his own helicopter charter service, he never had to experience the cold, he rarely if ever suffered a traffic jam, and the bureaucracy was negligible, at best. Being his own boss proved to be the only solution to sanity.

While based in the Keys, "Crunch" as he was known by his friends due to his habit of constantly cracking his knuckles, had a second outfit in Havana. The embargo had lifted, making doing business in this once heavily regulated country possible. Given that MasterCard and Netflix, as well as Google were all moving into the country, his job had grown quickly and showed no sign of slowing down. In fact, he was able to buy his second Chopper just this past year. Between his charter business—where tourists and professionals had been the lion share of his business, along with his more recent foray into aerial photography, which was going to become more profitable very quickly.

Peter decided to make Havana his main landing spot, because most of the business doors were opening there. However, during one weekend excursion with a certain lady friend last summer, he discovered Cienfuegos. This city of about 150,000 was a four hour drive, or in his case, about an 55 minute flight from the capital. He liked the city because of the beaches, the architecture, the food and the people. The fact that it also housed an adequate airport made the choice for occasional stopovers all the easier.

Today, he was shuttling a Toronto real estate developer and his girlfriend from Havana to Cienfuegos to look at the majestic and historical Cienfuegos Yacht Club. Inside word was that the developer-entrepreneur was going to plant the first Canadian flag to build a Spanish-modern high-rise on the adjacent property to the club. He was going to pump dozens of millions in order to stake his place among the first uber successful companies to help shift the face of this charming and historical city.

Just as Peter was preparing to fuel up before heading back to Havana for the night, he couldn't help but become distracted by an entourage of armed personnel, surrounding several civilians being forcefully invited to board two tricked-out, all-black Cadillac Escapades.

That's odd. Four soldiers. No—five, including the woman. She's no ordinary soldier. WAIT, I've seen two of those men before. They were talking to the waitress back at MIA. I overhead them talking. They were gassing up to head this way. Thing is, they looked in control then. They don't now. He tried to remain chill, not drawing attention to himself. He let his Maui Jim sunglasses and baseball cap keep him partially hidden.

What the—? Why is that soldier carrying a man over his shoulder? That doesn't look good.

Peter returned the hose to the pump, finished wiping down the front glass and headed toward the building to pay up. As he got closer, he tried to spot the license plates. Scorpion 1. And the other? Scorpion 2. That won't be hard to remember. Shit, I've heard about that character. Those must be his men. He's known to be deadly. That is his posse.

Peter walked into the office to run his card, keeping one eye on the group and the other on the person in front of him. Shit, one of them spotted me! It looked as though the man was heading toward him. After signing the receipt, Peter tosses the pen and heads back to his bird.

I don't need any trouble with these monsters, he thought. I'm sure it's all just...

Tap, Tap. Peter turns around, expecting to get punched in the face, only to be greeted by the young cuban attendant.

"Sorry sir. You forgot your receipt," the kid said in broken English, smiling and holding out the paper for Peter.

"Oh, okay. Thanks."

As Peter folded the receipt into his pocket, he watched the kid run back into the office, but couldn't see where the guy in all black had headed.

He was here a minute ago, he thinks, looking around. Nothing. Strange.

Climbing back into his Bell 407, something nags at him, so he double-checks all around him, opened his side window and called for an All Clear. Starting up the bird, he was running his last instrument check when a man, standing just outside his window, appears and startles Peter.

"Hey!" the man shouted, waving his arms in a downward motion to signify Wait.

Peter didn't cut the engines, but did pop the door open.

The man's steely gaze said, All business.

"Hi, I'm Steve." He extended his hand. Peter hesitated a second, then shook the stranger's hand.

"Peter. Cohen. What can I do you for?"

"Me and my buddies need to do some flyovers. We work in real estate development and wonder if we could hire you." His gaze didn't shift.

"Sure. When and where?"

"Well, today would be great," Steve said. "Like, maybe…now?"

Peter felt the skin crawl on the back of his skull.

"Yeah, I've got to make a run up to Havana," Peter replied, looking down at a clipboard on the co-pilot's seat. "I could do tomorrow."

The man didn't shift a muscle.

"Yeah, that's not gonna work. Any chance of your canceling your gig? We can pay."

Peter didn't flinch.

"Handsomely. And in cash," Steve shouted above the sound of the blades whirring overhead.

While that was always tempting, Peter felt fairly certain this had to be drug money. And once you take money that's tainted in that way...You're open to getting more than you bargain for.

Peter started to shake his head, when the man's hand slowly drifted down toward his side. It wasn't enough to warrant a full spook, but Peter certainly had to make a decision quickly. If he tried to lift off while the stranger stood on his platform, it would risk throwing the chopper off balance, or even worse, tossing him to the ground. Either move would cause repercussions Peter didn't want to face.

"Sure. What the hell, but I'm $600 an hour. Wet. That means fueled up and ready to fly."

The stranger nodded as to say I know.

"How much time you need?"

"Two, maybe three hours. Max," Steve said, shifting his gaze for the first time in the conversation. He looked over his shoulder in the direction of the two SUVs. His uniformed pals were standing at the ready by the vehicles, evidently awaiting a signal. Peter let his left hand slowly move to the seat pocket just below him. There, Peter kept a locked and loaded M-1911, loaded with .45 ACP. It was a standard issue sidearm for the U.S.A.F.

As the stranger turned back, he instantly noticed Peter's hand had shifted positions and started to reach for his gun. Peter redirected his hand and instead pulled up a small black notebook.

"Let's see..." Peter continued, looking through the notebook. It didn't seem like this guy would take no for an answer, but Peter would try anyway.

"Let me make a quick bounce up to Havana and back. I can easily be ready to roll in say...two hours? Maybe 90-minutes."

It was evident that was a push. This guy was getting impatient, and locked his stare.

"Let's call it $1200 an hour. I'll pay you for 4 hours...just as a buffer," he offered a small, if non-convincing smile. "Shut her down, I'll bring my visitors over, and I'll pay you now. "

That was hard to turn down. I'll make my week before dinner, Peter thought. Hell, I'll be fine. I've been in worse places.

"Done," Peter said, shutting down the turbos and nodding toward the passenger cabin, "As you can see, I seat four in the back and could squeeze in a fifth, but with extra luggage, I wouldn't suggest it. Plus..." he pats the seat, "this is the co-pilot's seat. How many you got?"

"Five. That's all we need," Steve says, turning to wave his pals over. He motions to one, pointing toward his ear. Peter assumed they were on a walkie system.

"Hold on; they're coming," Steve said to Peter and then radios to his team, "Parrot, grab Carter, his pal and the girl. We're a go. The others...just hold tight."

"Copy that," Parrot said in his ear.

"Any bags?" Peter asked.

"No. Short trip. Just down the coast. Know where the Juragua Nuclear Power Plant is?"

"Formerly Nuclear. Sure. Been abandoned forever. Back when the Russians and Cubans didn't want to play ball anymore."

"Yeah. Something like that. We're looking to convert it."

Peter found that odd, given it's been sitting for more than 20 years. What the hell; not my business, he thought, I'm just interested in making my nut for the month.

As the crew arrived, all the men had removed their visitors restraints, so as to not call attention to what was happening; however, all the crew had their guns exposed and ready to draw in an instant. Everyone knew what was expected.

Steve opens the doors and motions for Xeon to sit up front. "Birdman, help the lady up, won't you?" Birdman squeezes her arm to show he's got his eye on her. She smiles a mocking smile.

"Hi there. I'm Xeon. What's your name?" She instantly introduces herself, extending her hand and leaning close enough for him to smell her.

"Unique name. I'm Peter. Nice to meet you," he says, shaking her hand and enjoying her figure.

Birdman gives her arm a squeeze. She stops shaking Peter's hand and turns to her captor.

"Thank you, Mr. Birdman. I'm all tucked in now. Mr. Peter here will help me with my lap belt. You run along now, she says, pushing him back and pulling the door closed. Birdman lets it go.

"Mr. Carter," Steve says, "You join us in the back. Kindly sit directly behind Peter. That way you and I can discuss our real estate details...face to face."

"Uh huh," I say, climbing aboard and sitting with my back to the pilot.

"And Mr. Mack, you can sit here," he motions to the back, "This way, you and Parrot can chat among yourselves."

"Fuck you, very much," Mack says just loudly enough for Steve to hear it, then straps himself in, catty-corner to Carter.

Parrot climbs aboard, his back to Xeon. He immediately adjusts his seat so that he can slide his .9mm between the seats. He nudges the gun into her ribcage, just so she knows he's serious.

"OH" she says, not expecting that. "Are you playing tickle

with me, Mr. Parrot? You're such a playful and silly boy." She pats Peter's thigh, adding, "Are you a playful boy, Peter?"

"Uh, not...really," he stammers, "But I suppose I could," he winks, facing the dash to run his departure checklist.

Steve circles the helicopter and taps Peter's window. Peter jumps and turns to open the door. Steve pulls a thick roll of hundreds from his pants pocket. He pulls back the corner and flips through it to show they're all hundred dollar bills and hands it to Peter.

"Trust me, it's all there. And keep the change. Consider it a tip."

Peter nods. He likes this. Geez, $5,000 for less than a half days work. Not bad, he thinks, shoving the cash into his pocket.

As Steve climbs in and buckles up, he waves over one of the remaining crew, "Surfer, you, Ammo and Sparks take the Lieutenant and his buddy with you. We'll meet you shortly. Scorpion and the other team are easily there by now. We'll get there, set up and finish this when you arrive." He winks then says loudly, for Peter's benefit, "Peter's going to fly us over a couple of tracts of land, as well as the abandoned nuclear power plant so that we can see what's out there. We'll catch up with you and the others a little later. I'm anxious to see more of this beautiful country."

Surfer smiles, nods and is gone. Nearly to the SUV's, he waves for the others to mount up and move out. Peter starts up the massive twin turbo engines, lifts up and is gone in seconds.

I stare at Steve who returns the hard look and remains emotionless. I then check in with my pal. Mack is staring a hole through his bunkmate, Parrot. If it's a contest, I think, Mack will win every time. Mack breaks visual contact and looks to me, trying to figure a way to send a signal of his thoughts, without giving anything away. At this close proximity, it won't be easy, as Parrot is watching his every move. Same with Steve being glued to me.

While Xeon, in the front cabin, glances down to be sure her blouse is adequately revealing. Silly, but necessary, she muses to herself. She looks at the cyclic and says, "My, that's quite a shaft you have there, Peter." It's cheesy, but it works, she thinks. She imagines that Mack is rolling his eyes in the back seat, but secretly wishing he could be up front to get some distraction of his own.

After a few minutes of uncomfortable silence, I finally say something.

"So, Steve...about this property we're going to look at; do you think it's going to be the investment we all hope it will be?"

"I'm sure you'll be happy with whatever investment opportunity we provide. Look at it this way; we have something you want, we're pretty much in the driver seat, and we all know it."

Of course, I was being a smart-ass, but I think Steve may be playing along for no other reason but the mere entertainment value of the situation. Here's what I did know: we had less than 20 minutes to come up with some sort of plan whereby we had the upper hand; mainly because I had zero idea what Donovan had in store for all of us. And given his sadistic reputation, it could, without a doubt, turn out badly. After all, he didn't owe me anything. He didn't know me from Adam. And I doubt he knew that Randall and I were father and son.

As for Caprese, I know he had some bullshit ransom idea up his sleeve. But the one guy who would move heaven and earth to get him safe is the guy being held captive right alongside him: Tony Black. This idiot-box has a two-for-one special, I amuse myself.

I have to try to think like Caprese and Scorpion. What is the highest and best use of the five of us? Randall is a high-ranking officer, but he's getting close to retirement. Black is just a special ops executive assistant, who's a hired assassin like me, but with a head full of secrets. He is also the oldest one of the bunch, and has been shot in the foot, which will no doubt lead to something pretty bad down the line.

As far as Mack and I are concerned, we're practically retired ourselves; we're older than most and that cuts down on our value—although we are significantly skilled killing machines. What group of maniacs wouldn't like to have us on their team? However, they know we served our country and have a tried and true dedication to the cause—something they will never have.

And Xeon? She's smart as heck and certainly easy on the eyes, but she's belligerent, with a helluva mouth, and while's she's a good soldier, she's not a ruthless killer with our same motivations. That leaves her outside the game.

One to three things were certain: We were in the crosshairs. We had ended up in the wrong place at the wrong time. And it didn't look like we had a very substantial opportunity for salvation.

What is it that they want? Or, plan to do with us?

With less weapons than they have, less than ten minutes to land, and potentially less than twenty-hours to live, we were genuinely behind the eight ball.

11.

THE SURPRISE

SUNDAY, MAY 2 — 1724Z

One of the more prolific books I have ever read was one I devoured back in the early days of my training in the Corp. The lessons would forever change me. It would alter the way I viewed "the enemy." It would shift the way I considered defending myself and my country. And it would prove to be an invaluable resource for me in any number of situations. It was required reading once you arrived anywhere near the higher echelon of military management. And every one of the leaders had read it—at least once. The book was The Art of War by Sun Tzu.

There were dozens of quotes I committed to memory, but one that comes to mind right now is: "The supreme art of war is to subdue the enemy without fighting." And while that seems noble and likely enlightened, at this particular time I'm going to call bullshit on it—instead, calling on one of my favorites. It goes a little something like this:

"Let your plans be dark and impenetrable as night, and when you move, fall like a thunderbolt."
This would be my mantra inside the next 7 minutes. And while I don't know at this exact second what that thunderbolt will be—it will most certainly evolve in my mind very shortly.
It was evident something needed to happen soon, as a tide was about to crash the beach and it would undoubtedly be rough. The redeeming thought for me right now? Mack and I had been in much tougher places before. That was certain. Of course, we'd never been inside less than 30 square feet, facing two trained killers packing heat, while on our way to a desolate location where a notorious drug lord and his band of soldier-like killers are considering taking our lives and tossing them in the dirt of an abandoned nuclear power plant.
I have Steve sitting across from me with a .45, no doubt loaded with a high-grain, hollow point round, ballsy enough to put a hole straight through me, the two chairs between me and the pilot, including Peter and through the windshield..straight through to Gitmo, at the opposite end of the country.
Wait. They are soldiers. Not just drug dealers. But what's the connection? And what's Caprese got to do with it?
The other part of the trouble was that Steve's partner in crime was this Parrot character to my left. He had his right hand wrapped around a .9mm Glock which was pressed into the ribcage of my new team member in the front seat. While I am sure Xeon can handle herself, as I'd seen her perform her ass-kicking acrobatics in Nicaragua, that gun is likely pointed straight up into her heart. And I don't know how trigger-happy the clown at the other end of the

gun really is, but it's not a comfortable situation. In his left hand, the maniac holds an Emerson Karambit G10. It's a fixed blade knife used for close-quarter fights. It's sharper than most anything out there and is unstoppable once you put it into motion. This means that he can pull a trigger with his right hand, while making quick movements with his left hand, potentially slicing both me and Mack wide open with just two quick swipes; that is, if he's as good as a knife handler as Mack is.

The bonus to the equation for Xeon is two-fold: first, they didn't pat her all the way down; or else, they'd know she's wearing a midriff bulletproof vest. That will help. She also has more moves than a contortionist at a carnival.

"We're less than five away from the power plant, Steve," Peter the pilot chimes in. "I'll take us high and wide so you can get a good picture of the lay of the land. Then I'll get closer so you can see—"

"Shut the hell up, Peter. We aren't surveying property. You're going to land on the flat roof, just to the side of the prominent dome. You can't miss it."

"What? I thought—"

"I didn't pay you five-grand to think. Just to fly. Now, kindly shut the fuck up."

"Take it easy, Steve," I say, "He's just trying to help us find the right property for our next suburbanite neighborhood."

Steve looks at me like Don't be a jackass.

It's nice that Peter had the foresight to have us all put on headphones in order to be able to talk to one another. With the power of the engines, and the wind noise inside this small cabin, it would be impossible to hear anyone say anything. Good for us, I thought, as I instigated the first part of my distraction. Mack and I have created a number of signals through the years; here, I would punctuate certain words with a long blink. He'd pick up on it quickly.

"So...Steve, what's the plan. Good call on these headphone cords. Otherwise, I wouldn't be able to handle the sound. It's like a knife in my ear. Can you hear shit?" I say, adding a snarky grin just to piss him off. "Mind if I take off my boots? My feet are choking me." I reach down and touch my boot.

"Sit back!" Steve barks, not taking his eyes off me. He was unnerved—just not showing it.

"Okay, okay. Just trying to give the dogs some air."

What Steve doesn't see is that I've clicked a tiny latch on my right boot, popping a small, pointed and extremely sharp blade from the tip of my boot.

Mack picks up my words, then says, "Copy that. I don't know about you guys, but I got bad motion sickness."

"Me, too, come to think of it, Mack," Xeon says from the front seat.

"Hey, hold on," Peter nervously interjects, "We're almost there. There are bags in the seat pockets."

You know, there are two things every human walking the planet does but hates to be up close to—especially in close quarters; one, taking a shit. The other, is puking.

On cue, Mack starts to heave, a spark of a nervousness hits the eyes of our perps, and I shout, "Lucky Strikes!"

In a blink, we all fall into action.

In one fell swoop, I shove my foot up into the bottom of Steve's seat, allowing me to puncture his ass. He screams and I grab his gun. Unfortunately, it goes off, instantly deafening all of us.

Simultaneously, Mack jerks his headphones off and wraps

the cord around Parrot's hand, furiously redirecting the flashing blade into the man's own thigh. He screams, his trigger finger pulling and firing a round through the front window, just missing Xeon's ribcage. Luckily, she has the presence to pull the gun from his hand, breaking three fingers in the process. Not that it matters, because Mack was able to circumnavigate the razor sharp blade into a main artery. Parrot should bleed out in a matter of moments.

"Holy shit!" Peter yells, "I gotta put this bitch down!"

We keep moving.

Steve's gun, now in my hand, is shoved up under his throat, cocked and ready to pump lead up into his skull.

"Not going exactly as you'd planned, huh, Steve? I say, knowing his ass must be bleeding like a stuck pig.

We're dropping quickly, and not even close to our intended target.

Again, good for us.

12.

THE PLAN

SUNDAY, MAY 2 — 1757Z

Juragua Nuclear Power Plant was a nuclear power plant under construction in Cuba when a suspension was announced in 1992, following the collapse of the Soviet Union and the termination of Soviet economic aid to Cuba. Russia and Cuba sought third-country financing to complete the plant in the mid '90's, but in 2000 the two countries agreed to abandon the project. It has sat untouched since then. From the air, it looked kinda spooky; I won't lie.

Just think; we were this close to have that shit near the U.S., I thought. Now that I've had some time to process it, it makes total sense why Donovan would select this part of Cuba—and Cuba in general, to create a home-base from which to operate. Cuba was still stuck in the '50's. The country was looking for an influx of business. The location was perfect in that it was in a circle of activity whereby other countries were harvesting and/or creating a sizable amount of drugs.

But there had to be something else, I thought. Some other reason.

I had Peter do us a large. First, we bound and gagged Steve, zip-tying his wrists and ankles. I wanted to string him up like a calf roping competition, but that would mean we'd have to carry his sorry ass around, and I wasn't up to it. Too much dead weight. Yes, I did puncture his ass. And no, he won't be able to sit down, or take a proper shit for a very long time. But, he won't bleed to death. Speaking of dead weight, as for Parrot, or whatever his real name was, unfortunately, Donovan's team now numbers eleven. I was going to have Peter dump him in the ocean, just off the coast of Juragua, but frankly, the last thing I needed was to garner any more attention to me and my team. Not only that, I had an idea where—even in his current state, he could help us greatly. So, I had Peter skip the dumpster duty and instead land, dropping Mack, Xeon and myself on the ground somewhere along the perimeter of the power plant. After we scouted a good vantage point, he lowered the five of us. Mack and I grabbed Parrot and propped him up against a tree. He was bound and gagged, but looked like he was sleeping. Steve, on the other hand, was awake but probably wished he was sleeping off a bottle of vodka and pain pills. We gagged and bound him, then propped him against a nearby tree. Now that Steve and Parrot were under the protection of some scrub, we would be free and clear to maneuver, without the dead weight of two thugs; pun intended.

Caprese and Donovan still had Randall and Black and I wouldn't stop until I had them both under my watch. And

I wouldn't rest until I saw to it that Caprese either went away for a very long time, with no chance of release. Or, if it had to happen, I would put him in the ground, in whatever manner I deemed necessary.

I had Steve's .45, Mack had Parrot's .9mm and knife, and Peter lent Xeon his .45, but with the promise of her letting him take her out to dinner when this was all over. She smiled and said Of course. Whether or not she intended to follow through was an entirely different story.

Being this far south and this time of the summer, we still had another couple of hours before dark, but the light was certainly starting to change. Fortunately, Peter had water on board his bird, so we had enough to get and keep us hydrated here in the scrub of what looked to be nearly desert. I wasn't sure what we'd do without transpo, but didn't let that stop us. Why would it?

"Whaddya say we split up, just in case we run into those idiots without our seeing them first," I suggest.

"Yeah, thanks to those two jackasses, at least we can get a bead on their plans with their radios, when we get in closer range."

"Sounds like a plan," Mack replies. "How 'bout I swing North, Xeon head South, and you take it up the middle, Lucky."

"Good idea," I respond. "Given the spacing, you two take the radios and just keep an eye on me."

I knew we'd have to move fast, in case Tony was in worsening shape. I was afraid he may have to lose that foot.

We set out quickly and quietly, keeping our eyes on the horizon and our ears open for sounds of either their SUVs, or potentially another helicopter.

Caprese was impressed with Donovan's operation. There was no way you could tell from the air that this place was anything but abandoned. With ties to Hollywood, Donovan hired some out-of-work set designers to come out and create what he called false roofs. The architects and designers had created an elaborate structure of scaffolding that combined faux stone and mesh which looked exactly like dilapidated walls and rooflines, with see-through access from below; yet from the air, you couldn't spot it except with the most powerful of optics. From below, it looked like a movie set. Inside was literally acres of hydroponic labs and workstations where some of the most sophisticated equipment electronically created and monitored some of the highest grade marijuana, cocaine, ecstasy and heroin. It was literally the biggest drug manufacturing plant, under one roof, in the world. And given that there were any number of ways to get the wide variety of substances out worldwide—including boats, ships, helicopters and planes, it made Donovan's distribution the very finest.

On any given day, there were hundreds of millions of dollars worth of highly addictive chemicals created and exported. No wonder Donovan, aka Scorpion, would stop anything that got in his way; he was on course to be one of the richest men in the world. Part of the reason that Caprese had become friends with Donovan was because of two primary reasons. First, Caprese needed his financing. Even though Caprese was considered rich by many measures, he didn't have nearly the ability to find that level of wealth. Their serendipitous meeting at a cafe in Havana a half-dozen years ago made for interesting bunkmates, or rather, hangar mates. Secondly, Caprese could offer Donovan access to Washington, many offices of the government, and even the White House itself.

"I'm growing impatient with some of these dramatics, Caprese," Donovan calmly said, while looking over a thick folder of spreadsheets which his gorgeous Japanese executive assistant MoWang provided.

MoWang was also Donovan's part-time girlfriend. At 5-7 and 120 pounds of pure fitness, her chestnut eyes and superb figure hinted at supermodel, while her Phd from MIT in Bio-Chemistry and an undergrad double in Business and Accounting, made for a super brainiac. Donovan kept ultra close tabs on her, never allowing her to go anywhere without one of his best bodyguards. Moreover, their home was impenetrable.

"Understood. But please realize that the Lieutenant Colonel and his assistant have provided me broad access to the underpinnings of my nation's capital, as well as has brought you literally thousands of clients—high-level clients I might add, for a very long time."

Donovan looked at him with a look that bordered between contempt and appreciation. That confused Caprese on more than one occasion.

"Let's just figure out what we need to do...and do it. As far as I'm concerned, I've gotten what I need from him and not really sure I have any reason to keep him around. So..." Donovan trails off, walking away with MoWang. "I'll be back in twenty. Give me an answer then...or I'll have my own."

Caprese knew what that meant. Donovan wouldn't just shoot Randall or Black, but he would make them suffer an excruciating death of paralyzed agony. Donovan enjoyed sending the message, You don't fuck with Scorpion.

Donovan had a specific scorpion flown in from Israel, because most scorpions—contrary to popular belief, didn't kill you. All known scorpion species possess venom and use it to primarily kill or paralyze their prey, so that they can eat them. However, as a general rule they will kill their prey with brute force, if possible, as opposed to venom. The venom is a mixture of compounds. Of the more than thousand known species of scorpion, only 25 have venom that is deadly to humans. The number one killer is referred to as the Deathstalker, killing its victims within minutes. The Leiurus Quinquestriatus is the one that Scorpion uses on the people who turn on him, cheat him, steal from him, or all around piss him off.

Randall and Black were strapped once again to two chairs. However, this time, the chairs were the same kind they had in prisons—used for either torture, or lobotomies. It was like an electric chair, but without the electricity. Instead, this is where Scorpion would lock his "patients" into place, while administering his notorious scorpion torture.

Caprese was perplexed. On the one hand, if he didn't provide a solution that made Donovan feel confident keeping Randall and his assistant alive would help create future alliances, then Donovan would get rid of them, and leave Caprese without an ally. On the other hand, Donovan was partly correct; Caprese had used up Randall's worth. His connections were solid enough to have built Caprese a very handsome lifestyle. And he could live without having that resource.

Carter, on the other hand, had swept in during Caprese's last negotiation and killed his allies, along with some enormous potential for future alliances and a shot at a

White House position. Carter also nearly killed him, and he knew that Carter was the sort of man who would stop at absolutely nothing to get his way. He had heard of his reputation long ago, when drilling down on a deep and well-informed, yet notoriously secret document of top level military powerhouses.

The clock was ticking. The situation was escalating. And Caprese was contemplating.

Black was in need of attending. Randall was tired of the waiting. And Carter's crew was deploying.

13.

THE MESSAGE

SUNDAY, MAY 2 — 1828Z

USMC Sergeant Major Daniel Whitestone sat in his office. He was alone. His team and this office ran seven days a week. There were no three-day weekends. No holidays to speak of. And rare vacations. And even more rare—sick days. Today, everyone had gone home for the day. Whitestone sat at his massive mahogany desk staring at an email he sent to Carter Matheson well over a week ago.

Carter had called to confirm the intel he had received from this very office. It happened to be news that this Sergeant Major was not comfortable sending. Delivering bad news was never easy. And in the decades since he'd begun with the Corps, he never, ever felt good about delivering that sort of news.

He had known Lieutenant Colonel Randall Matheson his entire professional military career. They had seen action together. They had shared war stories—both of ex-wives and years of service to their country. They had been bunk mates in training, infantry mates in combat. They were close comrades and good friends. The best of friends.

Then why did I not only deliver this news, but not help my friend? Whitestone asked himself in the dimming light of day. He read the email again:

(0415Z, April 25) ATTENTION: Captain Carter Matheson, MARSOC — This message is to alert you that according to our latest Intel, your father, Lieutenant Colonel Randall Matheson, US Marine Corp, has been reported as Missing In Action. According to sources within our bureau, approximately 0100Z, after departing Costa Rican airspace, our office was alerted that they lost contact. Lieutenant Colonel Randall "Bulldog" Matheson, Sergeant Thomas "Tommy" Black and Jennifer "Xeon" Black, along with co-pilot, Officer Daniel "Spike" Jefferies, were all reported as missing when they did not arrive as planned to Miami International Airport. The group was scheduled to arrive 2 hours and 45 minutes later, after an estimated departure time of 1:04. The estimated arrival time was approximately 3:52. We understand you have been out of reach for the past several days, but we need you to contact our office immediately upon your return. Lieutenant Colonel Matheson's wife has been contacted, as well as Sergeant Black's wife. Please accept our sincere condolences and rest assured that we will leave no stone unturned before we find these four officers.

It was that last line that turned his stomach. Why? Because he had given his word: We will leave no stone unturned before we find these four officers.

It was the mantra by which ALL branches of the military

lived: Leave No Man Behind.

That's where I'm wrong, he thinks. Where I failed.

Carter had tried to contact him on a number of occasions, but Whitestone was either too busy or too engaged in any number of distractions. When Carter was finally able to contact him, he simply told him not to worry—that he would find his father if it was the last thing he did. And Whitestone had let it rest.

Whitestone did work to get some initial elements into motion, but when Carter caught wind of it, he barked at the Sergeant Major saying, Only help if you will really help me. Help if you will actually pull ALL the stops, Sir. Carter was angry, bitter, perhaps even hurt. It was one of the few times he'd ever seen Carter get riled up—much less speak disrespectfully to the Sergeant Major. But this wasn't any ordinary soldier. This was "Bulldog Matheson." He was one of the most decorated soldiers anyone had ever seen. Carter finished their conversation with something that haunts Whitestone to this day.

The last time I was told someone would help me and my men...the detail fell apart and good men died.

Whitestone never forgot those words. And as hard as he tried, he desperately wanted to push aside and bury a memory of several years ago. It was a situation that never should have gone south.

Carter and a small group of assassins, aka Delta Force, were working alongside Seal Team Six in Pakistan, after receiving intel on Bin Laden. This was nearly two years before Bin Laden was eventually found and killed during an early morning raid by the Navy's Seal Team Six. That operation was directed by the Central Intelligence Agency, and involved the U.S. Army Special Operations

Command's 160th Special Operations Airborne Division, along with CIA operatives. Carter was part of the original group of men ordered to find Bin Laden. And he got close several times. In fact, they were nearly on top of Bin Laden's camp when something went wrong. Carter and his men were discovered at the last minute and needed help to get out of a sticky predicament. Due to delayed, or confusing intel—either of which was a possibility, the clock ticked past the time of action, causing Carter and his men to be in a place of imminent danger. In the end, only Carter and Mack escaped alive. During an ambush, four of his teammates were killed and one another put on a life support until his death a year later. It was never made clear as to who dropped the ball, but all fingers seemed to point to someone inside Whitestone's office.

These situations had weighed heavy on Whitestone for years. On top of that, making matters even tougher, he—or rather the Corps, had lost Jerry in the process. Jerry couldn't take the guilt anymore—couldn't take the heat of scrutiny. And while Jerry's death was called a "heart attack," according to autopsy paperwork—no one really knows for sure.

There are any number of ways one can settle a score, Whitestone thought to himself.

Guilt's an evil bitch, he mused.

He checked his watch. Stood to pour himself a drink, then stared out the window at the darkening day. He was weighing his options—as the guilt weighed heavily on his conscience.

Finishing his drink, he stood there, looking at all the dozens of medals and awards that hung on the large walls of his impressive office. He admired the fine furniture he had collected all these years. His mind reflected upon all the faces of the friends that appeared in dozens of photographs through the years; several hung on the wall next to his medals, while others adorned a credenza across the stately room. He could nearly hear the voices of so many who had died over the years, while the voices of others had long faded with time—either to be forgotten or buried.

He looked at his handsome family: a wife of 20+ years and two grown sons, both of whom had followed in his father's footsteps and enrolled in the Corps right out of High School. He even smiled at a photograph of his golden lab, Spartacus, who had joined his master and a few of his master's pals—during a hunting expedition. One of those pals was Randall.

He set the glass down, opened his side desk drawer, and removed his 1911. He held it firmly in his hand, just staring at it and recalling all the damage it had done through the years. He smelled it—the smell of graphite and oil permeated his nostrils.

Whitehall nearly lost his breath, as he felt the pain of guilt and just couldn't take that pain any longer. Something had to be done. No matter who had to pay, or what lengths had to be scaled to provide a solution.

I did everything I could do to help my friend and his son.

Or, did I?

14.

THE AMBUSH

SUNDAY, MAY 2 — 1929Z

My crew and I were separated—something we didn't like to do very often. Fortunately, we were all trained expertly. We all had superior strength and sixth senses. And we had the physical power to withstand a great deal of pain and even more disappointment. However, leaving one another exposed and in harms way—that was not my favorite move.

Without my phone, or a walkie talkie, I feel like a lone wolf. Imagine that, I murmured to myself.

Checking my TAG, I see that it's approaching 7:30. It was considerably darker now than when my day began. I feel thoroughly worn out. I'm ridiculously hungry. And ready to grab my men and get the hell out of this country.

It was then I heard a snap. It seemed to be coming from about 40, maybe 60 yards away. I froze in my tracks, ducking slowly behind a scrubby bush.

Another snap. This time from about the same distance but in the opposite direction. Likely those two clowns, I think, Stay put…just in case.

The next sound was a familiar one. It was a small chirp—like a bird.

Mack. Good, I thought.

I returned the sound, waited a second for the other reply. It didn't come.

The sound from the opposite direction snapped again. There was no accompanying sound there. But if that were Xeon, she may not know it.

Then came Mack's return chirp. But it was different. Still the sound, but—

Snap. I spun around. Standing there was Mack, alongside an enormous man. Mack looked like a dwarf compared to this guy. A Heckler & Koch HK416 rifle was pointed at the side of Mack's head.

"Hey, Lucky; guess I'm not." Mack said, "This guy saw me a hundred yards ago."

"Shit," I say, "But where's—"

"Over here, Not so lucky…again!" comes a voice from the rattiest looking one of Donovan's bunch. He has some massive amount of hair piled on top of his head. A scar runs down the side of his face. And he, likewise, has an HK416 trained at the side of Xeon's face.

"Sorry, guys. Guess they saw us coming," Xeon said, sheepishly.

That was the first time I'd ever seen that expression. There is an innocent side to her, after all, I thought.

"Okay, Jarheads, let's move out," said the large one.

Static, followed by voices chirped across all our radios. "Long hair" touches his ear then speaks into his lapel,

"Copy that. On our way." Directing his attention to his gun-buddy, he adds, "Gorilla, let's zip these idiots."

"Gorilla?" I laugh. "That makes sense. Look at the size of him."

"No shit," Mack chimes in.

Gorilla smacks Mack by the side of his head with the butt of his gun. Mack instinctively swings at the ape, who grabs his fist in mid-air and twists Mack's arm behind him like he was a little old lady .

"Nice try," Gorilla barks, then proceeds to zip-tie Mack, who is trying to rub the blood from just above his eye.

"Every one of you guys have crazy nicknames?" I ask both of them—looking from one to the other.

"Yeah, Mon. He's Gorilla," the longhair says in a slight Rasta accent. "Our resident bodyguard and keeper of all things violent. I'm Sparks. I'm good with bombs…"

"What the fuck you doing, Sparks? This ain't story time. Let's get these p-punks back to the p-plant and let Scorpion decide what's next." He starts heading in that direction, adding, "Let's go!"

"Alright, alright. Just, you know…"

"Yeah, letting them know shit that doesn't p-pertain to them," Gorilla stammers.

"Hey, Gorilla. I think you're a p-pussy. What do you think of th-that!"

I couldn't help pick on him. Too easy.

He cuts me a look that says I'm gonna kill you, then adds, "Shut it, Carter. I'd just as soon bake you where you stand. You…" he stops.

About now is when I better realize some of Xeon's more exceptional attributes. And I don't mean her perfectly robust figure. She has a sense—sixth, or otherwise, that allows her to see the psychology of the moment. Either that, or her street smarts are keener than I imagined.

"Don't pay attention to these guys, Gorilla. They're idiots," she takes the lead in the direction of where we're heading. "I met them on my last mission and unfortunately got stuck with them. My boss, Caprese, hired me to hang with them and get intel." She spins around to make sure Gorilla got an eyeful of the robust breasts peeking from her blouse, then spins back around as if to play ball with them. "Maybe we can work together."

At that moment, you could see Gorilla give in for just a split second. That, and his buddy Sparks—share a glance that said Did you see those puppies. They both have a look in their eyes—one that all men know. It's a deer in the headlights look that says I wanna grab those.

That's all we needed, because the next couple of minutes was like a scene out of a Quentin Tarantino movie.

Just as Gorilla was cutting a look to Sparks, Mack drops to the ground and using his body as a fulcrum, launches his leg straight out and at just the correct angle, kicking in Gorilla's knee with everything he had. Gorilla drops to the ground. Trying to gain his balance, Mack spins around, picking up a large rock with both hands. The fact his hands were zipped together actually helped as there was no dropping the rock. As he came to the arc of his swing, his hands and accompanying rock come crashing down right on the back of his Gorilla-like neck, nearly crushing his spine.

At just the split second that Sparks attention gets diverted, Xeon performs the perfect round-about kick. Her leg was so high in the air, that Sparks had the chance to duck—which is what she instinctively wanted. However, she snaps the lower part of her leg forward with all her might, kicking him in the back of his head. Unfortunately, with the amount of dreadlocks he had, the blow, while powerful, wasn't as impactful as anticipated and he falls but staggers and starts to regain ground.

Simultaneously, I kick Gorilla in his groin just before he's able to stand up. He drops like a sack of sand. My next move completes Xeon's first one, as I leap in the air, coming down on the back of Spark's head—that's perfectly exposed to me, with a crushing blow of my elbow. As he's down on the ground trying to regain composure, I give him two blows to the rib cage. The first punch hits Spark's solar plexus, knocking the wind from his sails. The second one connects and snaps a couple lower ribs, likely puncturing his lung. It won't kill him, but he won't be running any wind sprints anytime soon. It was lucky that I was the only one who didn't have a guard right on top of me, or else I wouldn't have been able to get a piece of these idiots as I did.

Mack, Xeon and I stand over the two apes, admiring our work. Gorilla is out cold.

"Hell, he may be dead," I say.

Mack checks his pulse on the side of his neck. "No. He's still ticking. It's slow, but steady."

Xeon is standing over Sparks, checking his pulse. "Yeah, he's still with us. Just needs an oxygen tank."

"Yeah, these two will come around, but it'll likely take some time," I say, checking the horizon and my watch. "Tell you the truth, I'm surprised we're not surrounded yet."

"There's still time," Mack says quietly.

"Shut it, Mack,' Xeon says, scanning the perimeter. "It's

gonna be dark soon and we won't be able to see a damn thing."

"You're right. Let's zip these two and do the same as we did with the other two clowns."

Mack pulls zips from their pockets and radios from their belts. Xeon gathers the weapons and extra ammo from their packs, and while she's at it, takes the bullet proof vests from the two vics and hands them to us. We nod and gear up.

"We're loaded for bear now, boys," she smiles, holding up two HK416's, two tazers and two belts of ammo."

"Damn skippy," I say. Grabbing Mack's jaw, I turn his head to examine the damage. "Let me see your ugly mug, bro."

He pushes my hand away. "Get off. I'm fine. Just a scratch," he says, wiping blood from his face.

"Let me see," Xeon says, tending to him like a mother. He lets her do that. But then, he should; she's better at it. And softer.

"Okay, we're good," I say, "Plenty of ammo, dark is on the way—which will work to our favor, and..."

"AND we're this much closer to getting your dad and his pal back. Then maybe, we can get the hell outta here before the next shit storm hits," Mack says.

I look at him, but add nothing.

"Sorry, were you saying something important?" he grins.

"What you said, plus maybe one more thing," I return.

"What's that, Lucky?" Xeon says, finishing up Mack's forehead gash with a butterfly strip and a larger bandage.

"Four down and eight to go."

Mack and Xeon simultaneously say, "Boom!"

15.

THE RECIPROCATION

SUNDAY, MAY 2 — 1959Z

He held the worn book in his hand, admiring the wisdom that lies within. Flipping through the dog-eared pages, his eyes stop on one page in particular. Several lines are highlighted with a yellow marker; their pages, yellowed with the passage of time and use. It was his favorite quote from Sun Tzu's Art of War. The quote read: "If you know the enemy and know yourself, you need not fear the result of a hundred battles. If you know yourself but not the enemy, for every victory gained you will also suffer a defeat. If you know neither the enemy nor yourself, you will succumb in every battle."

Sergeant Major Daniel Whitestone knew several things: He knew the enemy. It was called Evil. And any hand that was raised against his country would have to, at the least, be maimed, and at best, destroyed. Furthermore, as ashamed of his past as he may be, At least I know myself, he pondered.

And with that, he put the 1911 in the worn leather holster that lived in the drawer he kept next to the gun. Placing it around his waist, he buckled it tight. Then, he took a fat cigar from the humidor that sat atop his desk and lit it with a small blue torch. After a few long drags and accompanying blows of thick blue-gray smoke, he smiled.

Pushing the button on his intercom, he barked, “Martin, get in here right now.”

“Yes, Sir,” responded an eager voice.

“And bring the Intel from Carter’s most recent location with you.”

“Yes, Sir.”

Within seconds, a uniformed assistant was standing perfectly erect at the front of Whitestone’s desk. He held a short stack of papers. Whitestone flipped through them, nodding constantly, then looked over his shoulder at the dark sky. Checking his watch, he sighed heavily.

“I don’t care what you have to do, or how you have to do it, but get me these three things right away.” He paused.

“First: I want a pilot and a plane on the tarmac, gassed up and ready to fly inside the next 30 minutes. I’m going to Cuba. Tonight.”

The soldier nods, writing the details down just in case. He looks up, “Cuba, Sir?”

“Yes. Havana, to be exact. I hear it’s lovely this time of year.” He grins, to lighten the mood for just an instant.

“Yes, of course, Sir.”

“Second: I want TWO Evac Helos stationed and at the ready at Miami International, STAT. Get me the Apache-64E and a Hind-E; the Mi-24. The former should provide the heat we need, while the latter will get us the speed we need to get in and out fast. AND...I want a private bird at Reagan. Doesn't have to be big, just fast. Oh, and you're going with me."

The assistant looks up. "Copy that. Sir?"

"Was that a question, son?"

"No, Sir. I mean, yes, it was. Sort of."

"Well, was it or wasn't it? And did you have other plans...that were perhaps more important than serving your country?"

"No, Sir. Perfect. No plans, and I'll have this done right away, and packed...uh, pronto. Sir."

"Most excellent." He checks his watch. "For clarification, make that no later than 22:00, for both Helo's."

"Copy that, Sir."

"As for me; I mean, us...I want to be in the air and passing over MIA before your mother sits down for dinner."

"Yes, Sir. 2200," he continues to write, then adds, "And the third?"

"Yes. The third. I suppose I may need to clear things with the Colonel. Let's hope I don't have to go any higher. But just in case I need all my bases covered..." he says, reaching for a piece of paper on his desk, "Pass this info along to him. Tell him if he has any questions, just to call," he pats his cellphone on the desk, "This puppy never sleeps."

"Yes, Sir. Affirmative on all three matters."

"Good. Now, get busy. I have a team of brave soldiers to rescue...and very little time in which to do it!"

Sergeant Major Whitestone's assistant had all the transportation elements arranged. A private jet was parked outside a private hangar on the perimeter of Ronald Reagan Washington National Airport. The pilot and co-pilot were prepping for takeoff while the Sergeant Major sat in the cabin, going over last minute details on the screen of his secure laptop. They would be departing in minutes. It's good to have people in high places, Whitestone thought to himself, recalling a short list of favors that were due him, thanks to decades of "personal service" he provided for those on the ladder above him.

Elsewhere, two military helicopters were en route to Miami International Airport where they would sit until given further instructions. They would be deployed in an instant and reach Havana airspace in no more than 46 minutes. No use rattling cages we don't need to rattle. That is, until it's time to rattle them, Whitestone muses to himself, thinking about having them sit quiet until the last possible minute. After all, he didn't know their exact whereabouts in Havana, but he certainly knew that was the last place they were seen and electronically spotted.

On board the Apache, were two pilots—both armed and prepared for combat. In the belly of the beast were two recon outfits of four men each. That totaled ten men, for what could be an all-out war. On board the Hind-E were two pilots and two soldiers in back. They were on board for assistance, when the time came for evacuation.

As Whitestone considered his plan, he couldn't help but contemplate a few other things. Opening a new browser window, he types in Merriam-Webster Dictionary. He then types a word. As the page loads, the description reads: Reciprocation: a mutual exchange; a return in kind, or of life value.

"That's it," he mumbles to himself. "A mutual exchange: one favor for another. One life for another."

Startled, Whitestone realized he had nodded off for

several moments. He rubbed his eyes, looked out the window to regain some form of clarity, then checked his watch to learn it had only been 15 minutes that he had been asleep. Once the adrenaline stopped pumping and the single malt scotch kicked in, he couldn't help but turn the engines off. It was then he realized that he'd been going non-stop for nearly 20 hours.

The Lear Jet 45XR he was traveling in maintained an airspeed of Mach .076, or roughly 520 miles per hour. With only four people, little luggage but plenty of fuel on board, they were estimated to reach Havana in less than 20 minutes.

Whitestone began a checklist of all the things he needed to do in these last few moments before he reached foreign soil. He needed to be on point to do everything he could to deliver what he had promised to do.

He reflected back to that email: We will leave no stone unturned before we find these four officers. That was priority One. Nothing else mattered. And as Whitestone had said, he would move heaven and earth to help these men—his close friend...and his son.

"What do you mean the Sergeant Major commandeered THREE AIRCRAFT?" shouted First Lieutenant Douglas Abrahamson. "What is that Officer trying to do...rescue an entire fleet?" Whitestone continues, sitting upright in his barcalounger, staring at nothing in particular.

"Yes, sir. As I explained, he's on a mission to rescue his..."

"I heard you the first time, son. I'm not deaf," the First Lieutenant said sharply. "It's late, that's a tall order, it came out of nowhere, he took it upon himself...Well, hells-bells, why am I explaining myself to you?"

"I'm not sure, Sir," Whitestone's assistant said quietly.

"That was rhetorical, son. Jesus, where do we get you kids..." Whitestone stopped to catch his breath. "Don't answer that. And pardon me son; it's just I was enjoying a relaxing night at home—the first in awhile and, well..." he stopped. "Just...do me this. Get him on the phone. Have him call me. And for the love of God, country and all that's holy, get him on the phone with me inside the next 20 minutes, or I'll have your ass and his job!" He slammed the phone down, shook his head and made his way to the wet bar across the room. "Of all the..." he stopped, snorted and then poured a bourbon.

After two sips, the blood pressure is lowered, his breathing has slowed, and all seems to be at peace. For the most part. Whitestone allowed his eyes to just drift across the vast den; a room that is handsomely appointed with all sorts of masculine items like rifles, animal heads mounted high on the walls, thick and expensive rugs under his feet, and a cabinet of medals and books. After checking his watch, he walked over to the largest bookcase in the house, opened the heavy leaded glass doors to observe several of his more recent purchases. Being an avid lover of history, and particularly when it comes to battles, he loves the strategy that goes into winning.

Some of the titles include: 100 Decisive Battles...The Fifteen Decisive Battles of the World: From Marathon to Waterloo...The Greatest War Stories Never Told...Moment of Battle: The Twenty Clashes That Changed the World...An Encyclopedia of Battles: Accounts of Over 1560 Battles from 1479 B.C. to the Present...50 Battles That Changed the World...The Seventy Great Battles in History.

His anger softening, his eyes scanned the next shelf, as he considered the hundreds and hundreds of hours he has enjoyed reading and studying the great minds who created the strategies that protected this country, other countries and people in general.

The next shelf held books such as: A Short History of the Civil War: Ordeal by Fire...Outnumbered: Incredible Stories of History's Most Surprising Battlefield Upsets...Masters of the Battlefield: Great Moments from the Classical Age to the Napoleonic Era...World's Greatest Generals: 10 Commanders Who Conquered Empires, Revolutionized Warfare and Changed History Forever.

Then his eye falls on one last favorite. His father instructed him to read it years ago, while still attending West Point. He takes it from the shelf, and sitting down his drink, flips open the pages. A bookmark, tucked into the middle of the book, falls out. His eye follows along an underlined inscription, and he smiles.

The phone rings, startling him.

"Yes," he said a bit calmer than just moments before, but still on edge due to the unknown.

"Hello, Sir. It's Sergeant Major..."

"I know who it is, Whitestone. I was expecting you. At ease, soldier."

"Yes, Sir. Thank you for allowing me this opportunity to discuss matters with you."

Abrahamson grins knowing what this mission means to this man and takes the time to be the shoulder to lean on when a man needs to express something of such grand importance.

"Go on."

The two men spoke for several minutes, sharing the importance of missions, strategizing the mechanics of protocols, and listening to one another share some of the more personal battles they'd faced in their illustrious careers. The most somber moment came when Whitestone quietly acknowledged the loss of Abrahamson's eldest son—a decorated soldier who lost his life last summer in a head-on collision with a drunk driver. After years of serving their country, both men understood the meaning of service and honor, but they also shared a profound appreciation for the love of a son.

In the end, The Sergeant Major got what he needed, the First Lieutenant got what he needed, and the results were not that disparate from one another.

In closing comments, they bid one another goodbye, wishing good health and Godspeed. Abrahamson, after a moment of reflection, returned to his library shelf, picking up his favorite book and read aloud the underlined quote.

Treat your men as you would your own beloved sons. And they will follow you into the deepest valley. – Sun Tzu, The Art of War

16.

THE DISRUPTION

SUNDAY, MAY 2 – 2028Z

The last rays of daylight hug the horizon. There's just enough light to outline the abandoned nuclear power plant, making our job of seeing the scope of the project easier, but not allowing us much else. The three of us were surprised at the size of the building and were amazed at how little light or activity seemed to be going on.

How could an entire international business be driven from this one abandoned location, I ask myself. In fact, there was only two lights on the entire compound: one small red beacon light atop a short tower on the furtherest point of the compound. More than likely, it verified the highest point on the property. That was helpful for keeping bypassing planes or helicopters from clipping the top of the monolithic dome. The other light looked to be an old street light, near the mouth of the compound. The pole was slightly crooked and was probably installed sometime in the ’50’s. We had all commented at one time or another how strange, yet nostalgic how Cuba appeared frozen in the 1950’s. The cars, the clothes, and much of the design was being retained from that period.

We slowly made our way to what looked like one of the main entrances. As our pulses quickened and tensions rose, we all seemed to be thinking the same thing at the same time. Let’s get in, get out with nobody hurt. We all took a deep breath and whispered, “Show time.”

“Thanks for retrieving the midgets from the pockets of those two idiots,” I say to Xeon.

She nodded, “It’s what I do. Go through men’s pockets...in search of their midgets.”

It was nervous energy. And it was good. It got a smile from both of us.

The clickers, or as we called them, midgets were tiny devices that allowed you to emit an odd yet distinct sound that would give your partners an idea of where you were. It was a consistent sound that kept you from having to speak, whistle or the like. It sounded like a muffled cricket—fairly innocuous but helpful, especially when traversing dark areas.

Taking them from our pockets, we tested them.

“Perfect,” I say, “Here’s what I’m thinking: Let’s travel in a loose pack, just not separated from one another like before. We certainly have enough heat now to handle whatever shit’s coming our way.”

Mack nods, but seems unusually quiet. I start to say something, but stop.

“Hey guys, I was gonna keep it a secret, but I found something in Spark’s pocket that I think may help. Evidently, he’s the explosives guy,” Xeon says.

"Why?" I ask.

"I found this brick in one leg pocket. And while I'm not a bomb chick, I'd say it's C4."

Mack nods, "Bingo."

That was a huge find. Mack was unusually quiet for that level of a discovery.

"You okay?" I ask.

He nods, then looks at Xeon, "What else?"

"Okay, in the other leg pocket was a flair. Only one, though."

"One is all it takes, if used right," I add.

"I bet he has plenty..." Mack adds, "Somewhere...in there," he adds, pointing to the building, then dropping his head and rubbing his eye.

"What is it?" I ask.

He doesn't say anything; just rubs his eye again and looks in the opposite direction.

"Mack. What is it?"

"Do you have a flashlight? I don't have one," he says.

"I do. Another thing I clipped from numb-nuts," Xeon says.

"Squat down and shine it on the ground. Please. It's dark and...well, I need to be sure about something," he says.

Xeon kneels down and shines the light directly to the ground, shielding it with her hand. He and I squat.

"Shit," he says.

Now, I've known Mack a long time. He's never complained once. When we were in Afghanistan, he got shot in the leg, diving in front of me, protecting me from a sniper's bullet. He couldn't walk right for six months. No complaints. Another time, we were on a boat off the coast of Hai Phong—miles from Hanoi, Vietnam's capital. We were on a recon gig, being shot at, when a piece of shrapnel came aboard. Without thinking, he picked it up and heaved it out to sea. Good news: we lived. Bad news: he had third degree burns on his throwing hand. It took several grafts and a dozen operations to make the hand right. Again, no complaints. I know Mack well enough to know when something's up and just pushed him one more time, this time, getting up in his face but without any words.

"I can't see out of my left eye," he whispers.

"What?" I blurt.

"Shit. I knew something wasn't right," Xeon adds.

"Yeah, guess that asshole hit me harder than I thought. It was blurry for a couple minutes, but then I got this sharp pain about 5 minutes ago—as we were making our way here. It just went dark..."

I wasn't sure what to say, but we knew one another too well to bullshit.

"Okay, as hard as this is to say, there's nothing we can do. Not now. But we will get the very best surgeon's on this. I promise," I say, smacking his shoulder.

He nods.

Xeon kisses his cheek. "Sorry, bruiser."

This soft moment seemed odd, what with all that was happening, but I didn't give a shit. Make that: what I did give a shit about was the fact I called him, again, for another mission. And he came, without a moment's hesitation. So, I owed him big. Again.

"Okay, let's cut this boo-hoo shit and go blow the fuckin' balls off these bastards...and rescue our guys!"

"That's what I'm talking about," I grin.

"You guys are so eloquent. And I see that sensitivity training those Marines gave you really does work!" she laughs.

Carter and his partners stay low and quickly make their way to the power plant. They should be up and inside in less than ten minutes, pending any complications or surprises.

What they weren't counting on was the fact that they'd been spotted just minutes ago—thanks to the tiny blip of light from what appeared to be a flashlight, and their every move was being observed on an extremely large screen inside, thanks to night vision assistance.

Scorpion watched with relish, eager to see these trespassers come face to face with the devil himself. He had such a wicked surprise in store for them. Turning to his captors, he grinned like a kid at Christmas. One of them stared back with a look of anger that could drop a man to their knees. The other, couldn't see anything at all; he hadn't been able to see anything for quite some time.

"Lights out, children," Scorpion said to his crew.

17.

THE DEPLOYMENT

SUNDAY, MAY 2 – 2059Z

The Sergeant Major's assistant, Charles Barber, quietly appeared and tapped his boss on the shoulder. Whitestone snapped out of his deep thought, looked up and motioned for him to sit down.

"What is it?" he asked his assistant.

Charles had been with Whitestone for nearly five years now, and in all that time, they'd never gotten in an argument. It was strictly a boss/employee relationship, so Charles knew his boundaries. In fact, he'd never been much for sharing an opinion except when specifically asked for one—which has been pretty much never. However, given that he'd also never traveled on a mission in all that time, and the fact that his life could now be in some imminent danger, he felt compelled—even confident, that now was the time to say something. Whitestone noticed the trepidation his employee was having and reacted accordingly, before he could speak.

"Look, Charles. I know this is tentative position I've put you in. And it's a bonus that for the past five years you haven't had to accompany on any sort of detail. Yours has pretty much been a desk job—although your job description states that you can be placed..."

"Sorry to interrupt, Sir, but I'm not coming to you to complain, or to express any sort of doubt, or fear...it's just that I wanted to say..." he hesitates, looking at the floor, then out the window.

"What is it, son. Spit it out."

"It's just that...I've always wanted to be a soldier. I've just never really had the opportunity. So, I wanted you to know that I'm prepared to do whatever it takes to help bring these men home. That's what I signed up for; whatever it takes to honor and protect the freedoms of our country. And their men. I just wanted you to know: no matter what happens...I've got your back. Sir."

Whitestone wasn't sure what to say. He was taken aback by this display of honor. It wasn't heroics; Whitestone knew Barber well enough to know that he wasn't sucking up, but instead was doing exactly what all good men did who really believed in being a part of the most honorable profession in which a man could enlist.

"Thank you, Charles."

Barber nodded, knowing this was perhaps the first time—in five years, that the Sergeant Major called him by his first name. He didn't take that moment of recognition lightly.

"I hope you know you're going to be fine. And I'm going to be fine. You know why? Because we have some of the brightest and best men on the planet willing to lay down their lives for their fellow men…just to be sure we are safe and their duty to our country is honored."

"Yes, Sir."

"Now, where are we?"

Charles checks his watch and says, "It should be less than ten minutes before we land at Jose Marti International Airport. Once there, I've orchestrated a meeting with local officials." He looks at his ever-present notepad, then continues, "An Officer Caesar Chavez will meet us. His men were the ones who located the car Carter and Mack rented. We're lucky the car wasn't stolen, and that Carter forgot the backpack—it had the beacon tracker sewn inside."

"Thanks for the update."

"Yes, of course, sir," Charles says, standing to resume his position in the back of the plane.

Whitestone holds up his hand to stop him. "Two quick things," Whitestone smiled, holding up an index finger, "First of all, Carter is the lucky one; thus his nickname. Secondly," he added second finger, "Carter did not forget his backpack. Either it was meant to be left behind, or he and Mack were abducted—which is my guess, given we haven't heard a peep from him. And yes, Carter should have checked in by now."

"Copy that, sir."

"One thing we know, Carter Matheson is on his father's trail. It's just a matter of time when he catches up to Randall. And with Mack by his side, it's a good chance they'll get what they need, when they need it…and in a quick stretch of time. This man doesn't waste much time when he has something on his mind."

"Yes, sir," he answers, walking to the back of the plane,

just as the co-pilot sticks his head out of the front cabin door.

"Please confirm you're buckled up, Sir. We'll have you set down at JMI in less than five minutes."

Whitestone nods to the co-pilot, locks his table tray into position, tightens his seatbelt and then crosses himself. Never hurts to pull in reinforcements, Whitestone thinks.

It had been hours since Peter took on a chopper full of strangers. What had begun as "a nice thing to do" nearly got him killed. And as much shit as he'd seen over the years, there was no reason to go back for more—even if it involved some civies. As far as I'm concerned, I saved their lives, he thinks.

Sitting in a comfortable chair in his comfortable efficiency apartment in Havana, Peter couldn't help but think about the time he'd spent in the U.S. Army, Airborne Division and how much he liked the camaraderie between his men. But when he was taken out of action after being shot down in a rescue mission, Peter took the medical leave and hung up his wings, thinking it was likely the best for his wife and himself. Neither his marriage, nor his tenure in the force had much of longevity. She left him two months before he was dispatched home. Peter should have seen it coming; she wasn't happy and always wanted a dumber and younger man—neither of those things could he do much about. As for the force, he had done his time, gotten injured, was released, and decided to enjoy a simpler life where he was in total control and could make the sort of living he wanted without having to answer to anyone. Flying his choppers between Miami, Key West and Havana proved to be the perfect recipe for success, and without the fear of dying on any given day.

Something was nagging at him. Peter was happy to help—especially given they were brothers in arms. He would have stuck around and done more. Hell, I lent that gal, Xeon, my .45! But he wondered if he would regret not doing more to help those people. Peter could have gone for help and could have dropped the men and just helped that Xeon. Man, she was beautiful. Wonder if she'd go out with me, Peter thought, realizing he hadn't been on a date in a long time. That body? Damn!

Peter sat there, running ideas through his head, one after another—ways he could do something. There were other ways he could help; like donate time to helping Vets enter retirement, there in Key West. Many guys dropped off the map, after not being able to locate a good job, or recover from broken marriages, rehabilitating themselves after bouts of alcohol and/or drugs. Sometimes the terrors just got the best of them—screwing with their minds.

Several moments passed and he got up and went to the kitchen. Standing there with the fridge wide open, he stared at a bag of salad that was past its prime, a meager collection of assorted condiments, a carton of milk he didn't remember opening, and a partially broken six-pack of beer. Peter began contemplating finishing the whole sixer after he poured himself a scotch. Or three. What the hell am I supposed to do? After all, I'm just ONE guy.

Peter walked back through the apartment to the tiny deck that hung off the side of his 3-story apartment building, overlooking downtown Havana. And waited.

"Fuck it," he says to the night, heads back in, locks the french doors, makes a quick change of clothes, transforming from shorts and a Hawaiian shirt wearing tourist to a Camo-wearing pilot. He grabs a backup .45 and a concealable .38 along with his Bug-out bag, and is out the door and in his Jeep in less time that it would have taken to polish off that partial six pack.

Checking his TAG Heuer watch, Peter figures he can be at the airport and airborne inside seven minutes; sooner, if he steps on it. Thoughts of Xeon and her pals makes his chest pound. Okay, she makes my heart race, he thinks, But the chance to help my brothers—that's what really gets my clock ticking.

The Sergeant Major, his assistant, and the two pilots touch down without incident. At the gate, they're greeted by Captain Caesar Chavez. The Captain has two Officers who stand armed and ready to assist, but not before checking credentials and going over a few notes—mainly, bylaws and protocols they must strictly follow in order to retain order. They make pleasantries before getting down to business.

"We're glad to help you and your men locate your missing team," Captain Chavez says in excellent English. "And while we don't get a good deal of American traffic these days—much less any military traffic, like I say, we are happy to assist."

"Thank you," Whitestone says, "We greatly appreciate it. As my assistant here explained, not only have my two men gone missing, but they were en route to find another two missing men—soldiers who were kidnapped while en route from Nicaragua."

This gets an odd look from all three Cuban officers. It's apparent to Whitestone that Chavez is trying to hide something—either an opinion, a secret, or intel. Whitestone was sure of only one thing: something was making him nervous, and he didn't like that feeling. He kept going.

"We're so grateful for your helping in this matter. As I'm sure you can appreciate, these men we need to rescue are all decorated soldiers who are of the highest caliber. The two higher ranking soldiers, Randall Matheson and Tony Black, share a braintrust of government secrets between the two of them; frankly, it's staggering. The other two men, Carter Matheson and Steve MacKenzie, are two of our top soldiers. Their credentials are also of the highest caliber, putting them in the upper echelon of special agents. Frankly, they are killing machines; two of the men we send in alongside teams like Seal Team Six, Delta Force...and others. Finally, there's an additional soldier, a woman code-named Xeon, who is one of our new secret weapons. Let's just say, gentlemen, she's a lethal dose of ass-kicking."

This gets a small laugh from the group.

"Seriously, I cannot stress how imperative it is we rescue these five."

They nod in agreement.

He continues by taking a manilla folder from his assistant and flips it open.

"Furthermore, there is new intel, we've just received from...well, let's just say inside our systems. It says both Carter and Mack may have been apprehended by a man with the name of..." He flips up a page to reveal a photo. "Donovan Blair, aka Scorpion."

Captain Chavez and his officers look at one another. The looks aren't encouraging.

"Sergeant Major, would you...please excuse me and my men for just a moment or two?"

Without waiting for an answer Chavez waves his officers

to join him several yards away, out of earshot.

There is an awkward silence while they wait.

"Well, I wasn't expecting that," Whitestone finally says, after several long moments.

Rushing to the airport, Peter Cohen checks his watch once again, nearly running a red light in the process. Shit! He screamed in his head, still running possible scenarios through his mind. Any number of situations could have occurred since last he saw those three. There's no telling where they are, what condition they're in, or what shit storm they could have dropped into. Peter knew that if he could get his chopper fueled and ready, he could be in Cienfuegos in less than twenty minutes. Where he'd land is an entirely different thing. He was trying to recall if there were any signs of life–as in lights in the area, so he'd know exactly where to put the bird down. Landing in the scrub is hard enough. Landing in the dark scrub is even worse. And the only thing that could top that shit storm is IF that abandoned power plant had anything to do with Scorpion...and vice versa.

Just as Peter was about to pull into the hangar area, he spotted a private jet and two police cars. From this distance, he couldn't tell, but it looked like the officers were escorting someone to their squad cars.

"That doesn't look promising," he said aloud.

The Sergeant Major knew he didn't like the feel of this situation, and this most recent idea from Captain Chavez pushed him over the edge.

"What do you mean you want to take us to your headquarters in order to fill out paperwork and orchestrate a rental car for us," Whitestone paused, wondering if these men thought that he was that ignorant.

"I'll just call a service."

The Captain and his men took one step forward, fully expecting them to comply.

They clearly were not.

Charles was on his cellphone and searching for a taxi, or any sort of car service that he could get at this hour and on this day. He was confident that his boss would expect him to do whatever it took to get them out of this situation.

"Sergeant Major, we are not interested in detaining you, it's simply that—"

A horn blows in the distance. All headed turn in that direction to see an oversized Jeep come speeding across the tarmac. Within seconds, it screeched to a halt. As a man jumped out the Jeep, the three officers along with Whitestone and Abrahamson looked at one another, then the approaching man.

"There you gentlemen are. I apologize for being so tardy," Peter continued, reading the group as quickly as he could, while ascertaining the players.

Locals. Check. Stripes; man in charge. Check. Nerd with briefcase; assistant. Check. The two men at the plane; pilots. Check.

"I see you missed the proper coordinates for our rendezvous. It was to be Cienfuegos, not Havana. Again, my apologies. HQ called, but I was on another errand. Please..." Peter motions toward his Jeep, while cordially smiling at the local police, being as polite as possible. He knows that if they wanted to, they could make things very complicated. Approaching the visitors, he motioned for them to join get in the Jeep.

"Come this way, Sergeant Major," he salutes. "I'm Sergeant Peter Cohen, U.S. Army, 82nd Airborne

Division."

Whitestone returned the salute, adding, "At ease, soldier. We just arrived from Washington..."

Whitestone quickly ascertains that this is the way to go, so he proceeded, waving for Charles to join in the ruse.

"Sergeant Major, I must insist that you consider the ramifications if you are to join this man and make your way to Cienfuegos," Captain Chavez said.

Chavez eyeballed Peter, assuming the man is legit, but trying to ascertain what his motives were. He reconsiders the situation, knowing they are about to enter a hopeless situation.

Captain Chavez had dealt with Scorpion on several occasions, and many of them ended poorly. In fact, several of his officers, who wanted to take it upon themselves to try and prove one point or another, didn't understand the depth of insanity with which they were trying to deal. Moreover, Chavez knew one thing for certain; a man like Scorpion wasn't going to be stopped. He was a sort of cockroach—one that, no matter how many times you stepped on his head, appeared to reappear again and again, duplicating and growing bigger and stronger, spreading his evil as far as a man's eye could see. Scorpion was all about greed. And the fuel of greed never seemed to run out. So, as his mind relived how many of those poorly orchestrated situations had ended, he ascertained that the only way to play, was to play along. After all, Captain Chavez and several of his men lived handsomely and were able to save for their futures, take their wives and girlfriends on exotic vacations. Their children would grow up and get a good education—perhaps even move to America. Some day. Yes, he had wanted to help these

American soldiers, but once again the arrogance from which they operated was always the same.

Who am I to stand in their way, Chavez thought. They will find out on their own. And it won't be good. With that, he nodded and waved them on their way.

No one spoke until they arrived on the other side of the tarmac where Peter's Bell Ranger was parked. Peter opened the doors and directed the two visitors to follow.

Opening a small baggage compartment for Charles, Peter said "Just toss your bags in this bay. And careful with the arsenal," he added, uncovering a cache of guns, ammo and several C4 bricks, "We may need some extra help," Peter then motions for Whitestone to climb inside.

"Sir, take that seat. Private, sit here, opposite him. And put those on," he said, pointing to the headsets. "Give me 90 seconds and we'll be on our way."

Peter moved around quickly, uncovering the intakes, running his hands along the rudders and performed a cursory check of his bird. Back inside, he turned on the instrument panels, shouted an All Clear out the window and started the chopper.

Lifting off, he says, "Okay, let me bring you gents up to speed. And I'll start by saying something you don't want to hear, but I'm sure you've ascertained. Your boys are in a world of shit."

"I am well aware of that," Whitestone said. "But what I don't understand is why Carter and Mack are not in Havana. Isn't this the last place they were spotted?"

"Yes. Shall I assume they were being tracked by your team?"

"Of course. We have a surveillance tracker on all our operatives."

"Well, he was intercepted by Scorpion's men yesterday and taken to a remote location in Cienfuegos. And when I say remote..."

"How can you be sure?" Whitestone asked.

"Because I took them there," Cohen replied.

Whitestone and Abrahamson look at one another.

"I was fueling up in Cienfuegos and heading back to Havana," he continued. "I share some hangar space there. Long story—not interesting, but I have a barter deal with this guy who's based out of DC. He's got a home in both Nicaragua and Havana."

Whitestone's attention is unwavering; he's catching every detail.

"Anyway, I run hops back and forth from the Keys and Havana, and also around the surrounding islands. It makes for a pretty good living. So, I was preparing to return to Havana when this guy, Steve, approaches me, asking to take him and some of his pals to Cienfuegos."

Whitestone nodded, while Abrahamson jotted occasional notes.

"This guy, Steve, brings along a pal of his. Both are dressed in all black. What's interesting is they both look military, or ex military. And with them, are two other men I happened to have seen at the Miami International Airport, last week."

"How coincidental," Whitestone said. "Or, fortuitous."

"I'll go with the latter," Cohen volleyed. "Anyway, I had seen these two and happened to overhear them talking about Havana...something about looking for someone...and such. All pretty interesting, huh?"

"Yes. Go on," Whitestone said.

"So, there we have two thugs, two strangers...except

there's one more 'soldier' in the form of a woman."

Whitestone nodded to Abrahamson.

"And a hot one, I might add. And this woman isn't afraid of anything. Big boobs...and balls to match," he chuckled, appreciating his own comment.

"Continue, Sergeant."

"Yes. Anyhow, fast forward. I know something's not right—I just don't know what's not right. I've got us heading to this power plant, right on the edge of the coast in..."

"In Juragua. The abandoned Nuclear Power Plant?" Whitestone interrupted.

"Yes, that's it. Why?"

"That power plant was started back in the late '70's; when Cuba and the Soviet Union signed an agreement to construct two 440-megawatt nuclear power reactors. They suspended construction in '92, when the Soviet Union collapsed, thus terminating the Soviet's economic aid to Cuba."

Whitestone hesitated a moment; he saw the pieces coming together.

"Shit!" Abrahamson said, adding, "Now, I see it."

Whitestone ignored him.

Cohen continued, "Well, your boys are some ass-kicking machines; they overpowered those two dudes on board—who were not amateurs, and had the situation in hand in a matter of minutes. They commandeered their weapons, along with one of my handguns, I put 'em down and then got the hell outta there."

He pointed to the two holes in the windshield that's been taped over. "Which explains these two holes. Suppose it could have ended up worse than it did."

"No shit," Charles spoke. Cohen looked at him.

"Just saying," he added.

Whitestone had been lost in thought, ignoring them, then said to Abrahamson, "So, that's got to be where Randall and Black are."

Peter chimed in, "That's where I left them."

"How long ago was that?"

Peter checked his watch. "Not 100%, but a solid guess puts it...inside 90 minutes?"

Whitestone does some quick calculations and turned to Abrahamson.

"Get Command on the line. Time to bring the thunder!"

18.

THE DIVERSION

SUNDAY, MAY 2 – 2111Z

Blade and Ammo stood on either side of Mack and myself, while Blade shadowed Xeon. All three captives were zip-tied, while the three captors were heavily armed. Blade, a knife and weapons specialist, was outfitted with an HK416, no less than 4 knives—strapped to both arms and both legs, while Ammo had a belt of explosives and also held a HK416, but with an extended clip. Wearing all black, along with their faces being painted black, it was easy to see how Carter and company hadn't seen them coming. It was evident that the men were not only experts in weapons, but they were extremely proficient in clandestine surveillance. Both stood, motionless, awaiting their next orders.

I was livid—not only because we had secured the upper hand not once but twice, but because we were this close to overtaking the power plant and commandeering Randall and Black. Both men looked terrible. If I didn't know better, I'd say that Black was already dead, as he was slumped over and his color was beyond pale.

Gangrene had to have set in by now, I thought to myself. Just hope he doesn't lose his foot.

As for Randall, he looked like he wasn't far behind. They were both tied to what looked to be electric chairs. Randall's wrists and ankles were secured with oversized leather belts, and his head was pulled back and attached to a post that came up through a support system in the back of the chair. His shirt had been ripped open, exposing his neck and chest.

Donovan and Caprese stood next to one another like old pals. Caprese's hand was on Randall's shoulder as though he was telling Randall a story. Next to Donovan stood a very attractive Japanese woman staring at a bank of computer screens. From where I stood, I couldn't see what she was looking at, but given the small group of people who also were watching a variety of screens, it was clear they were monitoring an elaborate project.

Hell, she could have been balancing her checkbook, for all I know, I thought.

What I did know was my father and Tony were on the edge of death and my number one job was to get them out of harms way and the hell out of here.

Scorpion saw the concern in my eyes. I could tell he was thoroughly enjoying the pain I was experiencing that very moment.

"We meet again, Carter," he says, grinning like a mad man. "I know—that sounds like a line from a James Bond film, doesn't it?" He asks, not expecting an answer. I give him one, nonetheless.

"Yes, it does, you sick prick. Although, I'm not sure you even understand film; especially being strung out on all the drugs you manufacture in this massive underground lab."

I enjoyed watching Donovan, aka Scorpion, display an expression of surprise.

"What makes you think that," he asks, knowing that I have an answer. He enjoyed the game he was playing.

"You have to know I'm on to you. You have to know that I knew this was all more that just about kidnapping." I have his attention. I continue, "We've been watching you for months."

His smile disappears, his eyes narrow, but he doesn't give me anything else. "You're full of shit and I'm empty of patience."

"Clever play on words, Donovan. You're a real wordsmith," I sneer. "In reality, Donovan, you're nothing but a drug-selling punk. Who just happens to be rich."

His face went blank.

"Actually, Carter, two corrections to your statement. First, I'm not just rich; I'm extremely rich. The sort of rich you could never even imagine. Secondly, I don't just sell drugs. I create alternate life experiences that..."

I interrupt, "Bullshit! You hook people on poison for your own gain. And in the meantime, you play chess with people's lives. Even Caprese's there. He's nothing but a ridiculous pawn in your chess game."

Caprese didn't like that; however, he didn't have the guts to do anything about it. He and I and everyone in the room knew that fact.

Donovan had evidently run out of steam, or an interest for what was transpiring here. He was clearly ready to make some sort of sizable move. And we were merely in his way. He nodded for one of his men to join him.

“Surfer, get me my pet.”

The guy he called Surfer looked just as you’d expect: long hair, deep tan, excellent physique, and, of course, dressed in all black, like everyone else. Reaching in a cabinet, he retrieved what looked like a miniature aquarium, but with a handle. It was darkly tinted and had a grate on the top.

I looked at Mack. His left eye was swollen and had hemorrhaged, causing the white part to be bright red. His other eye focused on me and blinked twice rapidly. This told me he was beginning a message.

He scanned the two guards on either side of us, looked at a nearby table, blinked twice, then to Randall and the stun gun on the table, blinked twice, then to Xeon’s belt, blinked twice, then to the guard next to him who had a long knife holstered on his calf. He came back on me, blinking twice—the end of the message. I followed his gaze and saw: scissors on a side table, the stun gun on the desk in front of Randall, then to Xeon’s belt where she had a small black tube—to the non-observant eye, it resembled a flashlight, but was instead a small twist of C4 explosive. I then saw the long serrated knife on the leg of one guard. I came back to meet his gaze and quickly blinked twice. Given that all eyes were on the glass cage that Surfer was handing to Donovan, all were oblivious to our code.

Donovan sat the clear box down. Because of the dark tint, I couldn’t see what was inside; however, because of his nickname, I had a pretty good idea of what it was.

“T-minus, 14 minutes until the target is in our sights,” Josh Borman said, double-checking a screen on the dash of his Mi-24M—code name: Hind E.

"Copy that, Eagle. I'm 3.5 seconds behind you," replied Scott Dowling, who was drafting Borman in the Apache AH-64E, a massive helicopter fitted with a mast mounted antenna with Longbow fire control radar. He turned to his co-pilot and nodded. He then flipped the safety covers on a single switch. This engaged the fire-and-forget mode of the Hellfire air-to-ground missiles. The 100-pound bombs would travel at Mach 3.1, or roughly 1,000 miles per hour, seeking its target without requiring line-of-sight. This meant that it could fly at night, through fog or smoke, before obliterating it.

Both helicopters—one set for evacuation purposes, and the other for destruction purposes would take care of both departments with one simple flip of the switch. The United States Armed Forces were nothing if prepared and completely ahead of the game in the ammunitions department; thus making them the strongest, most feared and most powerful forces in the free world.

Once they locked their targets, they could simply fire and forget, knowing the munitions would blow their targets straight to hell. Good news? Nothing would be left in the wake of the bombing for approximately a quarter mile radius. Bad news? If there was anything, or anyone that should not still be in the picture—they soon wouldn't be. Given that this team was not aware whether or not the area had Carter and his team, it was a precarious situation. They would just have to wait for further orders. What complicated matters further was that Carter currently didn't have any way to communicate with them; basically because he had no idea they were coming. As far as he was concerned, they were on their own. And since Peter

Cohen left in such a rush and without giving Carter even an inkling that he would be returning for them—again, he was on his own. This made the entire team nervous.

With less than 12 minutes to their targets, Borman and Dowling and their respective co-pilots were not only completely prepared to rescue their targets and then destroy whatever remaining targets needed to be annihilated, but more importantly, they were willing to die for whatever cause their country required of them.

On this particular night, the night was clear, the mission was even clearer and their focus was keen and precise. These men had never failed. And they weren't going to start tonight.

19.

THE COUNTDOWN

SUNDAY, MAY 2 — 2132Z

Mack and I had seen sticky situations before. You don't perform at the level we did without being in some serious shit storms. But this? We were in one of the most complicated places I ever recall.

Randall was tired, weak and appeared to be seconds away from being tortured, or worse: killed, by a method and by a man from whence he got his nickname—Scorpion.

Black, if not already dead, was certainly knocking on deaths' door. The only way I can imagine he'd been able to withstand this much pain was simple. He was one of the most decorated soldiers I'd ever met, and had more intel between his two ears than nearly anyone on the force. Black had been trained in some of the most evil and complicated torture practices any force had ever invented. And as part of that training, he had subjected himself to bits and pieces of said torture, just as a way for him to fully understand what people were capable of doing to one another. Not to mention the fact that he had seen entirely too many tours of duty in his life. Tony Black was, without a doubt, one tough son-of-a-bitch.

Then there's Mack, who was likewise one of the strongest and most determined men I'd ever known in my life. I'd seen him endure more pain than was imaginable. And now, here he was beat down, hungry, tired and blind in one eye. Two things were for sure: first, he and I would get out of this situation. Failure was not an option; I had no fear of that. Secondly, he and I were going to take the next month off. We'd disappear and not lift a finger for 30 days. That would be my first order of business; that is, once we got out of here in one piece.

That left Xeon. I had grown to like her—very quickly, in fact. More importantly, I had grown to admire and respect not only her strength and fortitude, but an attitude that didn't take any guff from anyone. Xeon thought like a man; concise, unemotional and matter of fact. No matter what it took—she, like we, would always survive. She was exceptional in martial arts, weapons and tactical. Bottom line: I had zero worry about her.

I looked at Mack and he, at me. We both understood the plan we'd put into action moments ago, and knew that in the next few seconds, we'd learn what we were made of. In fact, our precision was so tight that it may have as well been choreographed. The only hiccups I could see were as follows: while not considered insurmountable, the maneuvers would require rapid reflexes and impeccable timing.

First, Xeon wasn't aware of what we were about to do. However, she was imminently adaptable and I'd seen her on the fly acrobatics, hand-to-hand combat and her expert way with guns. She had a particular finesse that was fun to watch.

The second variable that would complicate matters was the fact that we had two men covering me and Mack, one covering Xeon, Donovan was loaded for bear and had his able-bodied assistant immediately beside him. Furthermore, there were two more armed and dangerous men in the room and no telling how many were nearby. Or were there?

So far, we'd killed the co-pilot they called Parrot, as well as Steve the boxer—aka Champ. Birdman, the other pilot, was also down. We'd disabled Gorilla the bodyguard and Sparks the bomb specialist. That's five down with seven to go. In front of us stood, Ammo the ammunitions guy, Blade the knife guy and Surfer, the water boy. That left three plus Donovan—rounding out the nasty dozen.

Where did they come up with these nicknames, I thought. I understand the need to be brief and clever, but some of them were laughable—even at this moment.

As Surfer delivered Donovan his "mystery box," I had an increasingly uncomfortable feeling that the heat in the room was about to get turned up a notch. And I don't mean temperature. I couldn't put my finger on that feeling I was having, but it was as though time were slowing down. There was a feeling of that eery calm just before a storm. And I didn't like it.

Josh Borman, Scott Dowling and Peter Cohen were flying in a triangular formation. They were now less than seven minutes from the target location in Cienfuegos. Cohen knew the approximate location, but given that the area was dark and had very little if any landing lights, plus the fact that it was edged right up next to the water, all made for a precarious situation.

"Gentlemen, we're close to our rendezvous. Due to lighting, or rather my lack of infrared like you guys have, I am kinda flying blind," Peter Cohen shared with the other two aircraft. "We're less than seven minutes from the nuclear power plant. I repeat..."

"We are less than seven minutes from the nuclear power plant," the voice on the radio repeated.

"What the hell is that?" barked Camo, the camouflage and surveillance expert. He was manning the bank of large screens that watched over the compound and the waterways nearby, as well as several that monitored thermo readings from anything that approached the compound. This way, they would be able to see anything that could not be seen with the naked eye. That was the beauty of infrared: the technology could detect any person or animal that emitted heat.

"Look! North of us, just off the coast, southeast of Cienaga de Zapata National Park," he added.

"Copy that," Pony the trainer said.

"Give me audio on anything you hear within a 20 mile radius," Camo added. "The minute you have a confirmed position and description of the aircraft, let me know so I can alert Scorpion."

"Copy. I've almost got it," Pony said, trying to keep him engaged while focusing in on the target.

"Wait, here it is," Pony added. "They're bearing is Northeast of us. ETA for arrival? Not sure, but I'm guessing five, maybe six minutes."

"I've got to tell Scorpion. Where's Numbers? I need him in here now. I want a count on the amount of processed materials that are ready to ship out tonight. Also, I need a confirmation of how many vessels will be used for shipping. Last: I need the HELO in the DOME gassed and ready NOW!"

A phone call came in just as Donovan was about to pull his pet out of its box. He stopped to take it. Personally, I think he's just toying with us. I'm not even sure why Donavan was taking the time to engage with us; I felt confident he had better things to do. It also made me wonder what Caprese had to do with this. What did the Doctor stand to gain? There must have been a bigger play in place with him.

Maybe Caprese was helping him move product, I thought. Maybe Caprese's relationships in and around Washington were more drug related than I thought. Isn't he all about the feeling of power that comes from controlling people around him?

He was looking at me right now, as though reading my thoughts. He stepped closer to Donovan who was clearly engrossed in the call, and looked over his shoulder to the paper he was reading. The one provided by the Asian gal pal.

What is he up to? I wonder, looking from Mack to Caprese and back, double-blinking to alert him.

Donovan's back was to Mack and I—he seemed to be trying to keep something from us. Caprese picked up the stun gun from the table, just as though it was perfectly normal. None of Donovan's men did a thing.

That's weird. Something's up.

Caprese was approaching us. He had evil in his eye. Or was it something else?

I looked to my right to see two men running down a long hallway, heading straight for us.

"Men, heads up," Cohen said to Borman and Dowling. "ETA is less than three minutes away. Given that we aren't 100-percent sure that Carter, Mack and Xeon are on the premises, we need to hang back." They were getting very close to being right on top of the power plant.

"Copy that," reported Borman.

"Copy that," repeated Dowling.

Caprese was within two feet of me when he looked at the guard watching me and frowned, nodding his head to imply Give me some room. He then leaned over pretending to check that my wrists were still engaged. What he whispered next, nearly made me shout.

"Men, we are within 200 yards of the power plant. See the red beacon on that short tower?" Cohen asked.

"Copy" is spoken simultaneously from both pilots.

"I'm circling around to the southernmost point. You two remain here off the coast, until I get a better eye on things. Click to copy."

Two double-clicks from both men confirmed receipt.

Caprese was so close I could smell his breath. It wasn't pleasant. "Carter, get me out of here alive and I'll turn myself in and see you're handsomely rewarded," he whispers.

Just then, two men ran in the room. A look of panic plastered their faces. This made the other guards nervous. They approached Donovan. While one handed him a sheet of paper, the other spoke in a low voice that I could't hear. "WHAT THE FUCK?" Donovan shouted across the room. The sudden outburst was such a departure from his ordinary cold and calculated self. The room stood still, awaiting his next move.

Donovan whipped his head toward me. I'll admit it—my stomach sank.

This room was about to explode in one of several ways: Donovan was going to release some sort of evil on either Black and/or Randall...Donovan was going to pull a gun and blow us all off the planet and go about his business, or...

"Cohen, this is Borman. Do you see what I'm seeing? Over."

"You mean the plant's dome opening like the Griffith Observatory?"

"Copy."

"Looks like it could be either a powerful telescope, a surface to air missile, or..."

Donovan looked from me, to his men, to the screens on the wall. I can't believe I hadn't noticed it before, but the entire room now saw two objects in the air, just off the coast.

"ARE THOSE YOURS, CARTER?" Donovan shouted.

Given the fact they were in a holding pattern, I had a feeling there were two helicopters. One of them had to be Cohen. He did come back, I thought. I didn't say anything; just stared.

An alert sounded. All heads turned to another screen. Another camera—the infrared one, was showing a helicopter landing on the opposite part of the compound. Within seconds, heat mass left the chopper and ran toward the building.

Wait. Cohen? That's three? What was he up to? I wonder if...

I looked at Donovan. He was confused and fuming. I just

smiled again. He wasn't amused.
He checked his watch, then picked up his clear box, reached inside and pulled out the largest scorpion I'd ever seen.
"Carter, there any 1750 species of scorpions. And while most people think they are all deadly. In fact, only 25 have the sort of venom that can kill a man. Death can be painful, if not debilitating."
He walked over to Black and held it nearly against his neck and watched me.
"Of those 25, only the top 5 provide an excrutiating death. It's an ugly thing to watch."
I didn't move.
"Especially if that someone—was a person you cared about. You'd do just about anything to stop the pain," he added, relishing the verbal torture.
I didn't budge a muscle.
"My little friend, here, is one of those top 5," Donovan sneered.
Again, I just waited to see his bluff. And to get this show going. Likewise, Donovan did nothing. I eyeballed Mack, who showed no emotion, but turned his head further than normal so as to see me with his good eye. We knew there was no turning back.
I looked back to Donovan and said, "You're insane, Donovan. Sorry, I mean, Scorpion. Ooooh...such a scary name" I added for affect, knowing that each moment that ticked pissed him further, but then, I'm just an asshole like that.
He took two steps back and held his pet over the head of Randall. My father ignored Donovan; his look to me said, Don't worry. I'll be fine, kid.

I could feel my blood boil.

Okay, now you're fucking with me, I thought, but didn't give him the satisfaction of seeing any change in emotion. Donovan smiled, then slowly pulled Randall's shirt open and dropped it in.

Within seconds, Randall screamed.

By now, Peter had made his way to the perimeter of the power plant, in just enough time to drop several balls of Playdough—our nickname for C4, around the edge of the exit doors. Within seconds, he was making his way to the rim of the roof which was now open. Peter heard the gunfire before he felt the bullets fly by his head by the dozen. Ducking, he had to get out of there fast. In order to detonate these explosives, the range was only several hundred yards. If he could make it back to his chopper, things should end fine.

"Borman, Dowling, I need help," Peter spoke softly into his mic.

"Copy. What can I do?" Borman asked.

"You need to stay put—just watch that roof. I can't see what's in there. Give me 60 seconds to get out of the way," Cohen said, "Dowling, you see where my bird is?"

"Copy that."

"Split from Borman and head that way. I'm going to need your help."

"Copy."

BOOM!

Either a grenade launcher, a surface to air missile, or something like that rocketed from the lip of the plant dome and was heading straight for the loaded Apache.

"I don't give a damn what you men have to do but you had better drop every one of those fucking birds out of the sky, or I'm going to shoot each of you in the head!" Scorpion shouted at the top of his lungs.

Randall was writhing in pain and already foaming at the mouth.

Donovan stood there, nearly dazed, enjoying the spectacle of my father reaching for his breath.

Fuck this, I thought, looking at Mack and then to Xeon. I nodded at Caprese who had inched his way back to the center of attention. While Mack and I had a plan in motion, I now had one extra ace up my sleeve.

That's when I yelled, "LUCKY STRIKES!"

Borman had the best electronics in the business. He'd been in the force longer than many of us. And his reactions were the fastest of anyone we'd ever seen.

He managed to pull up and away at the very last second—at just the right time.

"Holy shit!" Cohen screamed into his mic. "Well, at least it's not laser equipped, otherwise..."

BOOM!

All heads turned to see Peter's helicopter blow into bits.

The moment I yelled my charge, it disarmed the guards for a split second, which was just enough time for me to spin around, head-butt the dork guarding me. I spun around, grabbing the knife from his leg holster, split the zip tie with one move, while swinging around and went for his jugular. He'd bleed out by the time I crossed the room for Donovan.

Simultaneously, Mack pulled his duck-n-kick move, where he dropped to the ground, spun around and kicked the guards knee completely out of joint. Disabled, this threw the soon-to-be-cripple off balance. He dropped his gun. Mack picked it up and returned the favor, taking the butt of the gun and crushing the man's face. Mack then shot him in the chest for good measure.

Xeon had orchestrated her move perfectly. Dropping down, she caused her guard to lean forward, as though to reach over and grab her. What he wasn't expecting was her head coming up into his chin at full force. This, for all practical purposes, drove his head back so violently, it snapped his neck, causing him to fall like a bag of rocks.

Bringing those three men down, left only two, plus Donovan.

"Okay, guys. We know our men are here. Now, I'm a sitting duck," Cohen shouted, brushing himself off from dirt and debris that blew over him during the explosion. He knew that however fast he thought he needed to move, it hadn't been fast enough. The good news was that there weren't as many soldiers inside as Peter had originally predicted. In fact, given the lack of massive firepower, he estimated that quite likely only one or two men were at the helm of this recent shooting.

"Borman, give me enough time to get inside," Peter continued. "The minute I call it, blow this place to hell."

"Copy that, Cohen," Borman shouted. "I've got you."

"Dowling, stand by, you're going to be our escape."

"Copy," said, Dowling. "I'll be on the backside of the plant and ready to pull you out."

In the seconds that passed, Donovan obviously had made an executive decision: Fuck everyone and get to the roof. He slung an HK over his shoulder and headed up a winding staircase across the room.

It was his next move that surprised me.

Donovan pulled a .45 from his belt and aimed it directly at Caprese, then he hesitated and returned it to his side. The look on his face was quizzical. Donovan reached for the hand of his Asian assistant, and the expression on her face went from hatred to admiration in a blink. Sprinting up the stairs, they disappeared through a door that obviously led to the roof.

The thunderous sound of a helicopter boomed above us. I couldn't do anything about it at that moment. Instead, I looked to Mack, threw him the Tazer gun Caprese had slipped me and nodded in Donovan's direction.

I ran toward to Randall who was slumped over and passed out. Strangely enough, Caprese had cut Black loose and was reaching toward Randall with a knife in one hand and reaching in his pocket with the other. I grabbed his wrist.

"Carter, I'm on your side. Just give me a second." Caprese retrieved a small sealed vial with a built-in syringe from his pocket.

"What the hell?" I said.

"I never trusted that maniac Donovan. As soon as I learned his moves, I created a back-up plan. Just in case he turned on me. This antidote should help."

"Should?" I shouted.

"Will," Caprese said, pushing my hand aside, popping the cap on the vial and preparing to shove it into Randall's thigh.

We looked at one another—not completely sure what to do next. His eyes gave me the answer: Trust me.

Xeon, had taken it upon herself to run down a long hall to what she assumed was their Command Center. The red lights all along the corridor were flashing and the overhead alarms were deafening, setting the entire complex on full alert. As she arrived at the mouth of a monstrous room, workers were scattering like roaches, heading for escape doors. Xeon ignored them, instead, turning her attention to Donovan's clandestine drug factory. Being underground had allowed him to create a behemoth laboratory, far from wandering eyes. It was a brilliant and very sophisticated network of special lighting, ventilation and hydroponics. Has to be the largest self-contained marijuana factory I've ever seen, she thought. Her eyes scanned the room and landed on an enormous kiln of some sort. Moving closer, Xeon look inside, shaking her head. There, she saw hundreds of thousands, if not millions of brightly colored pills. Reaching in, she pulled out a handful of tiny pills. Embossed on each was a skull and crossbones adorned with rabbit ears. It was a deadly, yet happy juxtaposition. Xeon had seen this logo before, but couldn't place where that was.

Ecstasy, she whispered, adding, No wonder.

Randall's nearly non-existent heartbeat was slowly returning, while Caprese and I were quickly running out of time.

That's when it hit me: They're gonna blow this place!

"Quick, can you pull him around?" I said to Caprese.

"Of course."

As if on cue, Randall coughed up blood and opened his eyes wide, gasping for air.

I exhaled a deep breath of relief, grabbed Caprese's shoulder and said, "I owe you."

He nodded, but said nothing.

"And Black?" I added, not waiting for an answer; instead, running to the screens.

"I'm not a miracle worker, but I'll try," shouted Caprese to my back.

Approaching the large screens, I saw one helicopter in the air. It was still in the same space.
Gotta be an Apache, I surmised. Performing calculations with my watch, I tried to speculate how much fuel he had left. He would be draining it by the dozens of gallons with every second he hung in space.
"Caprese, get those men out of there!" I shouted, running toward the hall that Xeon had disappeared into. I shouted, "Xeon!"
Within seconds, she came sprinting around a corner and was in front of me, breathless.
"Do you have any idea what's down that hall," she asked, pointing in the opposite direction.
"I have to believe either drugs or ammo," I answered, grabbing her by the arm and moving her toward the exit.
Caprese had gotten Randall to his feet and the two of them were putting Black's arms over their shoulders, carrying his nearly dead weight toward the exit.
An alarm sounded overhead, followed by a mechanical voice that said, "3 minutes to detonation. 3 minutes to detonation."
We look at one another. At the same time, we say "What the..."
BOOM!

The blast that came next was Donovan's chopper launching a missile at Borman's helicopter. He, too, had an Apache AH-64. Fortunately, Donovan's pilot was not as experienced as Borman.
At 58 feet in length and 15 feet in height, and with a travel speed of just under 185 miles per hour, this $50-million killing machine was a force to be reckoned with. And with two of them within several hundred yards of the same

airspace, it had the potential to be a deadly rain of steel and artillery.

Donovan had no immediate interest in getting into a air assault, outside of showing that he wasn't going to be intimidated. His primary concern was getting the hell out of there. Which he did, inside five seconds.

Peter was coming down the iron steps, just as my team were successfully exiting the building rooftop. We could see from this vantage point his burning helicopter to our south, our Apache still in the air, to the north, and Donovan's chopper hightailing it toward the west.

"We gotta move NOW!" I shouted, asking Peter, "Where are we?"

"We have an Evac chopper there," he pointed to behind us, to the East. "Our guys have Randall and Black on board. Whaddya say we smoke this place?"

"Perfect. Got room for all of us?" I smile, for the first time today.

"Of course," Peter replies. "Let's go," he says, turning and heading toward the chopper. "The minute you give me the word, we'll torch it."

"Carter!" Xeon says, grabbing my arm. "What's with Caprese?" she asks, watching Peter's men help him load Randall and Black.

"Long story. More later."

We started to dash when I realized, I was missing something amidst all the chaos.

"Where the hell is Mack?" I shout in the direction of Xeon and Peter.

"WHAT?" she replies?, "I assumed he was with–" she turns to Peter.

He shakes his head and says, "I thought he was with you!"

This realization makes my mind nearly explode. I whip my head toward Donovan's disappearing helicopter.

Time stood still. The helicopter blades were whooshing in slow motion. Xeon's distraught face stared at me, frozen in space. Peter shook his head in disbelief.

I snapped back.

"There's no way that Donovan would let this place stand a chance of getting confiscated. He's rigged it to blow. BUT...Mack may still be in there."

My mind was racing. I needed an answer. Randall and Tony were safe. Mission accomplished. But there was no way I was going to leave Mack behind, if he was still inside. And if Donovan had taken him...

"Peter, you and Xeon get our guys out of here. Get your Apache to change positions over the dome. I'm going back in and see if Mack's there." I wave for them to keep walking toward the chopper. "Get me a flare. The minute I find what I need, I'll fire it. Your boys can swoop down and get me, we'll blow the place to kingdom come and head out after Mack."

"NO fucking way!" Xeon shouts. "If you're so Lucky, then I'm going with you."

Before I can argue, she's grabbing the flare from Peter's grip and sprinting toward the building.

The alarm sounded again, just as we reached the lip of the tower.

"2 minutes to detonation. 2 minutes to detonation." The mechanical voice stated.

The building was clearly abandoned. No sign of Mack anywhere. My stomach turned. My heart sank. But my adrenaline was coursing through my body like a meteor shower.

"1 minute to detonation. 1 minute to detonation," the synthesized voice proclaimed overhead.

"We gotta get the fuck outta here, Lucky!" Xeon screams amidst the blaring sirens. The expression on her face was a mixture of pure fear and unadulterated determination to not let the current situation keep us from winning.

I hesitate.

"45, 44, 43..."

"Let's GO!" she shouts, as my head whips back and forth scanning the power plant, searching for an answer.

"39, 38, 37...

Mack had to be aboard that chopper. How would we ever...

"33, 32, 31...

Xeon was pulling at my arm. It was as though my mind was stopping me from moving forward. Donovan would surely kill my best friend. There is NO way he would let him live.

"27, 26, 25..."

I shook my head. Tears filled my eyes. I was paralyzed.

"22, 21, 20..."

I had to go. WE had to go. Peter was jumping up and down, waving his arms furiously. I could just hear him from across the way, "Let's get out of here!"

"18, 17, 16..."

"LET'S FUCKING GO!" Xeon shouts for the last time, then turns to sprint toward the helicopter, knowing I would follow.

"13, 12, 11...

I sprint toward the others and, slamming into the door, shout, "Peter, call them in!" as Xeon and I board.

He nods, grabs the mic and shouts, "Give me 5 seconds and UNLOAD!"

"8, 7, 6..."

We lift off, and just out of reach, Peter shouts "BURN IT!"
"3, 2, 1..."
BOOM! BOOOM! BOOOOM!

20.

THE AFTERMATH

SUNDAY, MAY 2 – 2344Z

It had been two hours since our Apache fired on the abandoned nuclear power plant. As if the explosives Donovan had set to blow the lab weren't enough, the addition of the four Hydra 70mm air-to-ground rockets and one AIM-92 Stinger finished off the location. It leveled 90% of the above-surface building, and likely more than half of what was left below. One thing was certain; no business would be conducted from this location, ever again.

Our entire team—two choppers, went after Donovan's Apache. We flew for as long as we could before we got close to running out of fuel. It was then we had to return to Havana. I saw to it that Randall and Black were admitted to a local hospital and attended to. Randall would be fine, thanks to the fast thinking of Caprese. Black had gone too far in seeing that his foot got the attention it needed. Doctors were doing everything they could to return him to health; however, it was possible he could lose the foot that Caprese shot. When he finally came to, matters would be explained, but I wasn't sure how Tony was going to handle things, or Caprese, for that matter. As far as I was concerned, I didn't know how I was going to explain to anyone in particular, but I owed Caprese, and I owed him large. I told him that we would pick things up when I returned.

We had put out an All Points Bulletin for Donovan, his crew—which were largely unknown to us, and of course, Mack. We didn't know who the pilot was, nor who the additional crew was that flew with Donovan. All we knew for certain was that not much was left behind in the wake of the explosions.

The one thing I knew for certain was that Mack was MIA and once again, we were left in the dark as to the details. Not since my father went missing, have I been so distraught. Mack was like a brother to me. He was actually more than a brother. Yes, I had a brother. His name is Jonathan; a pastor with a family, back home in Mission Grove, North Carolina. And while we were close, I've never had such a deep and intense relationship with another man as I had with Mack. If there were ever anything such as a soulmate between two men—this would be it. To say I'd move heaven and earth to find him, was an understatement.

It was late. I was flat-out exhausted. I hadn't slept or eaten in I don't know how long. So, as much as every fiber of my being wanted to set out on my next reconnaissance mission, I simply couldn't. I couldn't do it physically. I certainly couldn't do it mentally. I need food and sleep.

It was just past midnight by the time we had our guys checked in and settled into the hotel downtown. Caprese, of all people, suggested the Iberostar Parque Central Hotel. In fact, he insisted on setting us up and paying for the entire crew to stay there. It was a 5-star joint, so while I cared more about the whereabouts of my best pal, I agreed to stay. Might as well be comfortable as not. I told Xeon to get some rest and be ready to head out anytime between 0700 and 0800, tomorrow.

Having Caprese "on our side" felt incredibly crazy—what with all we'd been through, but the more I thought about it, the more it made sense. I told him goodnight, saying that I would circle back around first thing in the morning. He assured me that everything would be taken care of. He bid us goodnight and we all disbanded.

It took me a good half hour before I could get to sleep. The adrenaline had been surging through my body for so long that it took two rums to slow me down. While waiting to adjust to the quiet, I ran any number of facts and scenarios—in no particular order, through my cluttered mind.

Donovan and Caprese began our journey by kidnapping my father and Black. And while Donovan made me feel as though we were "simply in the way of his operations," he seemed to take a personal pleasure in seeing to it that our team suffered. In all reality, we didn't have anything against him. I mean, we could have come and gone and not given two shits about his drug trafficking business. The only part that I did mind was if he was sending said traffic into the States—which I had to assume he was. That bothered me; I didn't like the thought of my country getting polluted or destroyed by men who just wanted to make more and more money. On a slightly contradictory note, if he were "polluting" other countries, then so be it. I know—it didn't make much sense, but with all the sleep and food depravation, perhaps that was just it.

Caprese was still a confusing chess piece in this game. He had clearly been maneuvering people in positions in the White House. His driving passion was of a thirst for power. And while that's one of the oldest motivating factors of all time—it wasn't the end of the world. What he did inside the White House was actually a job. However, it was what he was trying to do outside the White House—with other countries, all of whom had nothing but corruption on their minds—was what screwed with my head. The bottom line with Caprese was that he could have let Randall, Tony, Mack, Xeon and myself all go down. He could have stepped aside and allowed Donovan to bury us all. But he didn't. Instead, not only did he step up and become an aide to us all in our moment of danger, but he saved my father's life. That's not lost on me. Nor will I let him burn for it. Truth be told, there was nothing he was actually doing wrong from the moment we showed up until now. Well, except he did shoot Tony in the foot. But as I analyze matters, I see why he did it. It could have been part of a ruse. It could have been part of a play. It could have also been a distraction—at Tony's expense. Not everyone wins in battle. We all knew that.

Back to Donovan. Something keeps knocking at the back of my mind. It has to do with the fact that Donovan's team was—or, rather is, so goddamned buttoned up. They are soldiers. Just look at them. Look at the way they operated. Look at their maneuvers. The fact that Mack, Xeon and I were able to overtake them didn't really matter that much.

After all, we are—and I say this to myself, we are superior soldiers. We are among the most elite in the world. That meant something. And what it really meant was—in all reality, it would be nearly impossible to overtake us. We'd just seen and done and learned and mastered too much.

So, what did that mean? Where were they trained? What were they trained for? This wasn't just a few guys outfitted with the very finest of weapons, selling illicit drugs to thugs around the world. This wasn't a battalion of hardened criminals making up some new type of corps.

Or, were they? Were they an inside group? Did they have some sort of new mission? Were they a clandestine operation that I didn't know about?

These questions raced through my mind at breakneck speed. I was confused. I was exhausted. I need sleep, I thought. I need to recharge and start out fresh, I thought.

The best news was that I had reached out to my contacts in Washington and they had an APB on Mack. This way, I could rest easier knowing the strongest minds in the business were on top of matters.

The singular fact that nagged at the back of my head was, What if Donovan shot Mack while getting into the Apache, pulled him aboard and just dumped his body somewhere between Cienfuegos and the Cayman Islands, or between here and Jamaica, or who knows where?

The only thing that rattled around in my gourd that was worse was, What if Donovan still had him and was going to torture him like he did with Randall?

If he had tossed him overboard, at least he would have died in peace.

Screw that! I thought. I'm going to find him...if it takes the very last breath I breathe. And with that, I let go and fell asleep.

21.

THE REGROUP

MONDAY, MAY 3 — 0644Z

A tap at the door disturbed the morning. Upon awakening, it took several moments before I fully knew where I was. I felt as though I'd been kicked by a mule. My head throbbed—no doubt, thanks to the rum. My body ached—thanks to chasing, hitting and getting hit. My stomach growled—must have been the lack of sufficient food over the past 72 hours. And my head twitched—from the inside out, thanks to the nagging suggestions that things weren't as they seemed. This thought would follow me the rest of the day.

Before answering the door, I looked around for my gun. It was on the dresser. I heard a familiar voice whisper in the crack of the door. It was Xeon. I left the gun and opened the door. She was wearing short shorts, a workout bra, and running shoes. Damn, I thought.

"Hey, Lucky. Wanna hit the gym before we head out?"

she asked, making her way in and walking to the wet bar. Pulling out a bottled water, she drank it while waiting for my answer.

Looking down at my fitted boxers, I said, "Uh, are you shitting me? We just got pummeled within an inch of our lives, and you…"

"Oh, shut it. That's the difference between men and boys, I suppose," she smiled, turning to leave.

"I mean…"

"Nah, I see you're still waking up. I'll just grab a quick couple miles on the treadmill down in the spa and meet you for breakfast on the veranda in say…" she said, checking her TAG. "How's 45 minutes? That enough time to down your vitamins and pills and…"

"Really?" I interrupt, smacking her bottom on her way out the door, "Go burn that nervous energy. I'll see you at breakfast."

Xeon looked at me and starts to speak, but I shut the door before she could reply.

I could hear her muttering, as she walked down the hall, but disregarded it, knowing I needed to get moving before taking off for Donovan. This was going to be a helluva day.

I was downstairs and in the dining hall two minutes before Xeon. Caprese was already there, showered and perfectly coiffed, as though he had been on a month long vacation.

"Morning," I said quietly, preferring to enter the day in a much more subtle way than I had previously.

"Good morning, Carter," Caprese replied, nodding for a nearby attendant to bring a fresh pot of coffee and fresh-squeezed juice.

I nodded to the waiter and didn't waste a moment

downing a cup of black coffee before Caprese could finish his morning greetings.

"I took the liberty of reaching out to some of my contacts," Caprese said, stopping to watch both an attractive Xeon and a well-worn Peter approach our table. He continues, standing to pull out a chair for Xeon, "My, you look most fetching, Xeon."

She smiled and took a seat.

"What about me" Peter asked, reaching for a coffee.

"Thank you for saving my life yesterday," Caprese says, before continuing with me.

"Think nothing of it. Another day at the office," Peter smiles.

"As I was saying, I reached out to some of my constituents here in Havana to...let's just say, aide us in our upcoming endeavors. I think you'll find them most helpful." Caprese checked his watch. "I've been assured that they can meet us at the airport in 30 minutes. That is, if that works for you."

I was still trying my best to get used to the thoughts of Caprese being on our side. Perhaps I had been wrong all along, but then again, he was a masterful competitor. He may have all sorts of plays up his sleeve.

"Frankly, Caprese, I'll, I mean we, will take any and all the help we can get. You know how much getting Mack back home means to me...and to this team. We're all inseparable. Well, we are now, anyway." I grin at both Xeon and Peter.

Peter chimes in. "I gotta tell you, Carter, it feels good to be in the shit again." He was scarfing scrambled eggs within an inch of his life.

"Yeah, kinda addictive, huh?" I reply, turning to Xeon for

confirmation.

"Copy that," she says, adding, "And with teammates like this one..." she points to me, "You gotta be on your game, or get your ass handed to you."

It took us all of an hour to get fueled, geared and gassed up and over to Jose Marti International Airport. As much as I wanted to get out of this country, catching a flight to just about anywhere but here, I would never sleep again without knowing the safety of Mack. Given that Peter's helicopter was destroyed by Donovan's men, and his second and smaller chopper wouldn't accommodate all of us and our equipment, I worked my magic to get Borman and Dowling to hang with us an extra several days until we located Mack. The other helicopter—the one used primarily for Evac, was sent back to Washington. My contacts in DC had no problem lending me the Apache for whatever purposes I had. They got their private Leer jet back; after all, the hourly rate on that puppy could eat up my yearly salary in just a matter of weeks.

We arrived just shy of 0900, and prepared to meet with Caprese's contacts. I had him briefly fill us in on what we could expect. First, I wanted to know their exact working relationship. He described in thorough detail—abandoning any preconceptions that I cared to bring him to any form of justice. As far as Caprese was concerned, when I said I owe you—that provided free and carte blanche access to all the Intel that was required for us to "get down to business" and pull all the strings that needed to be pulled in order to relocate Steve MacKenzie.

His men showed up promptly at nine. They were professional, cordial and extremely gracious and efficient in all manners of business. If I didn't know better, I would have sworn that they were Certified Public Accountants and not certifiably proficient annihilators—aka Hired Killers. They didn't just specialize in killing. Their supreme specialty was international banking; primarily counterfeit money. Their sub-specialty was ensconced in arms dealing; aka ammunitions. And their "gravy" on top was drugs; primarily, MDMA.

Bingo, I thought, relating the MDMA, aka Ecstasy to Donovan. They quickly explained that their allegiance was either to the highest bidder, or the longest relationship—whichever came first and provided the best return. Having a long-standing relationship with Caprese proved to be, once again, invaluable to all our matters at hand. I had to admire Caprese for his clever ingenuity and superlative focus. While he was less than trustworthy, he was proving to be worthy of my patience. And I suppose that this would certainly do. For now.

Inside the next 30 minutes, we formulated a plan that included mapping out a strategy as to where we would head first, what we would be doing and in what order, how we would manage to diminish the amount of time between Mack's capture and his retrieval. After all, we knew the longer the period between kidnap and return, the worse the chances of his being alive. Of course, when you're dealing with a cutthroat killer and drug dealer that pretty much abandoned the rest of his team in the blink of an eye, in order to save his own bacon; well, that was a good sign that he wouldn't be looking out for the best interest of all those involved.

It was quickly decided that we would start at the point where we lost Mack. That way, we figured we'd at least get a good handle on any clues we may have missed. With the Apache on call for the duration of our stay, we'd be able to make it to Cienfuegos in less than 50 minutes. In that time, we'd call on any other favors that Caprese would lead us to. He had already learned that Donovan had two locations for his drug factories. I safely assumed that Cienfuegos was the number one place. However, there was also a location in Jamaica. That trip would take considerably longer to navigate. Needless to say, we were ready to do just that. But something was nagging at me. I had the sneaking suspicion that the other side of Cuba may be a close alternative.

Given that we had some time to get to Cienfuegos, I called one of my old pals in Washington. His name was Jacques Hamner. We called him Jack Hammer because the joke was just too easy to miss. He was one of the sharpest minds in the business when it came to drug trafficking, and had been a junky at one time, so he had a visceral knowledge of the potential devastation of drugs. After doing some rehab, he decided to join the force. Mack and I had met him about ten years ago, while doing some undercover work in Manhattan. Jack was our liaison and proved to be not only a nice guy, but an invaluable asset in learning the tricks of the trade.

I left a message with his office and had a return call inside ten minutes. Jack had always been quick to return a call, and was willing to go the extra mile in helping a fellow officer create a solution to a problem. Calling him Jack Hammer was not lost on the fact that he was able to get in, find the worst of the worst and come crashing down on any cartel in the free world. Jack would prove to be a valuable asset in helping us locate Donovan.

Our phone conversation was being scrambled and

encrypted, so nobody anywhere would be able to hear the chat. Not that we worried about it, but it was certainly nice to know that we could rest assured we were safe from prying ears.

"Hey, Jack. Long time no see," I say.

"Yeah, Lucky. Good to hear from you. You still dating that surgeon from Carolina?"

"Funny how you'd recall that. And funny you should say that. In fact, yes; we saw one another not that long ago. Guess you could say that we reconnected. And the union was, well, quite nice."

We instantly picked up where we left off nearly a year ago, carrying on with pleasantries for nearly twenty minutes, catching up on girls, guns and all sorts of familiar shared interests, before we got down to business.

"Look, Jack, we're going to set down in Cienfuegos—the place Mack was abducted, in less than ten minutes, so we're going to have to cut to the chase."

"Copy that, Lucky. Just tell me what I need to do in order to help. You know how much I like Mack. He's one of the good guys. And you guys both—well, you helped me on more than a dozen occasions, you just tell me what I need to do and I'm there."

"Good. Thank you. First of all, we both know Donovan's drug of choice is MDMA..."

"Yeah, ecstasy. It's a bitch, bro. Highly addictive. Cheap to make. Easy to copy. Easier to manufacture. Completely painless to move across borders. And well...it's not expensive to make these days, if you're the type who doesn't mind stretching it out in order to make for higher margins."

"Copy that. He's also a big fan of marijuana. And why not;

some of the best is grown just south of us, in Jamaica. However, he's become the best in the business when it comes to hydroponics. His outfit is top drawer. He's also, I'm told, mastering a new super strain."

"Yeah, let me interrupt you there. We are just now learning about some of this. It's super tight; uh, super strong. It's getting a lot of pub on the streets. Most importantly, it's pulling in the highest dollars ever. I mean, it's being called the new cocaine. And the reason is because it's way cheaper than coke, it's equally as powerful, in some instances. Then again, it could just be another fad. My money? It's a toss up between the super strain and the new tabs—sorry, I mean the X."

"Agreed. We're all up to speed on that. No pun intended," I joked. "Here's what I really need to know. Does he have any major routes in DC, that you know of? And...before you answer, does this ring a bell?"

"What's that?"

"As far as you know, does he have any military background?"

There was long pause on the line before Jack continued.

"Lucky, can I put you on hold just 30 seconds?"

"Sure. I'll hold," I say, wondering what was coming next.

Exactly 30 seconds later, he returned to the line.

"Sorry, pal. I had to grab a file from an office mate. I think you're going to want to hear this. And for the record, it's really funny—strange maybe, that you should mention a military background."

That same strange feeling had been banging at the back of my head for a while now. I couldn't help saying, "I'm all ears."

22.

THE CIRCUMVENTION

MONDAY, MAY 3 — 1052Z

We landed in Cienfuegos without incident and immediately set out to track down any clues that could lead us to Mack. We knew we had to move quickly, so in the interest of time and energy, we split up. Cohen and Borman covered one part of the recently flattened former nuclear power plant where Donovan had been creating millions of dollars worth of drugs. Xeon and I took the other. In less than thirty minutes, we had covered what was remaining of the plant. Borman's barrage of missiles spent little time destroying nearly everything in sight. Oddly enough, a good portion of the dome remained, while all the surrounding walls and ancillary buildings were flattened. Underground, the vast majority of the laboratory was destroyed. Most of the damage was due to one of the two tunnels giving in on themselves, while much of the product had been turned to dust. I was damn glad. While this certainly wouldn't deter a man of Donovan's character, it would go a long way in slowing him down.

"I can't even manage an educated guess, about the volume of product going out of here on a weekly basis," I said.

Xeon was knee-deep in rubble, intently focusing on what looked to be a heavier than normal filing cabinet. "Well, I saw the machine in action, and while I don't have any real idea..." she stops and turns to me, "I'd have to wager a guess of in the millions." She smiled, returning to her dig.

"Very helpful, funny girl."

Things are looking absolutely futile when I hear Xeon grunt a sound that appears hopeful.

"What is it?"

"Come over here and make yourself useful," she said, pointing for me to help her upright a fallen safe. "Seems like something we should look into, huh?" she asked, not waiting for an answer, but instead retrieving a cellphone from her pants and dialing a number.

"You wanna tell me..." I start.

"Shut it. I'm trying to..." she interrupts, holding her hand up, "Hey John, it's Xeon. Good, good. How are you? Listen, I'm on a case and really pressed for time. I need you to run a search for me. Yes, I'll hold."

I was calculating a way to use leverage in order to stand it up, when she put her cell on speakerphone and helped me get it upright by the time John reconnected.

"Xeon?" the voice on the phone starts.

"Yeah?"

"Okay, let me guess what it is. A safe, right?" he asked.

"Yup, it's an old Winchester," she replied, stepping back to eyeball it for measurements. "It's 6 feet tall, I'd say 4 wide and just a bit less deep. Weighs a ton, blah-blah…"

"Okay, two things: first, tell me if it has a cowboy riding a horse on the front, with the word Legacy. Secondly, get me the serial number off the back."

"Yes, to the cowboy and legacy…" she walks around the back. "Don't see any serial. Either scratched off, or painted over. Plus, the light's not the best in here."

"No worries. That's enough. I'm checking my database. Give me 60 seconds."

I catch myself frowning.

"So, am I to assume you either used to be a thief, or currently are one?"

"Both," she said, coy as ever.

"Xeon, you have an Android, right?"

"Affirmative."

"Good. Check your email in 30 seconds. Click the link. Download the app. Type in your standard info, plus the 11 digit code that'll be attached the email. Once you have that, immediately place the phone over the lock's nose. Hold it until the app does its thing. You'll hear a triple beep. Then read me the sequence on your screen. I'll be able to assist from here, thanks to the programmable electronic lock."

"Copy that," she says, turning to me, "You get all that?"

"Just get started," I nod, "And I'll help you along."

She starts the process and is waiting for the app to complete the download when I lean toward her cellphone.

"Hi, John. It's Carter Matheson."

"Oh. Hi, Carter. Heard a lot about you. They call you Lucky, right?"

"Something like that. Anyway, tell me; this puppy has an auxiliary relocker, doesn't it? As in, doesn't our tampering with the lock activate the relocker into position, pretty much preventing entry?"

"Look at you. You been holding out on me?" Xeon asks, looking over her shoulder, adding a punch to my ribs for extra effect.

"Yeah, correct to the relocker; however, what I'm going to do with Jen, I mean Xeon, is to override it. It's simple. We should have it cracked in a matter of minutes."

We look at one another but say nothing. It's getting hotter under ground, and the clock is ticking. I'm trusting that her intuition is leading her to something that will crack this code. Pun intended.

After succinct instructions by him, a few adept maneuvers by her crafty fingertips, we are opening the heavy steel and titanium door of the one-ton beast. Our heads whipped toward one another then back to the contents.

Cohen and Borman leaned against the Apache, staring off into the distance. Borman was furiously chewing gum. Peter turned to him and asked, "You mad at that gum?"

"Huh?" Borman absently responded. "Why?"

"Because you're chewing the hell out of it."

This got a chuckle.

"Just trying to put myself inside Donovan's head," Borman said, staring out toward the horizon.

"Scary thought. But I get it. Been doing the same thing," Cohen said "I have an idea. How about you?"

"Well, way I see it is this: they made a nearly clean getaway. Meaning, as far as we know, Mack was actually on board the chopper when they escaped. Barely, I might add," he said, scratching his stubbly chin. "I still don't know how he diverted my missile."

Cohen patted his shoulder. "Lucky on his part. And to

your point, I have to believe he did make it off. I'm nearly positive that Donovan will be playing yet another kidnap move. With the Intel that Mack has in his gourd, he's certainly a valuable asset to Donovan. That is, if," he replied, adding air quotes, "The Scorpion knows what he has as a captive."

"True."

"What are your other thoughts?" Cohen asked, lighting a cigarette.

"We have a pretty good idea Jamaica's a second home base. And to confirm that, we could make that our next move. It's a quick flight. I get topped off, we bounce to Kingston and start there. I'm sure Carter will have Intel on his movements in Jamaica by the time we hit 10,000 feet."

Cohen nodded with no reply.

They're silent for several moments, before Borman spoke.

"My other thought?"

Cohen looked at him.

"Personally, I don't think he's in Jamaica."

Cohen raises his eyebrows.

"My money says he's in another part of this country."

"Ya think?"

"Cuba's not that big," he said, holding up his index finger. "780 miles long by 120 miles wide, that's 43,000 square miles," he continued, holding up a second finger. "It's got plenty of opportunities. While..." he held up a third finger, "Still having perfect, moderately monitored passageway for doing business...as in exporting his goods and services."

After a long pause, Peter tossed his cigarette butt then said, "You've been thinking about this, huh?"

"Since the call came for me to get down here. Did a little

R&D on Scorpion, checked in with some of my DC contacts about the trafficking trade that we've been watching for some time. And I knew that if Lucky Matheson's on the job; well, I'd best be as up on things as possible."

Peter snorted, "No doubt."

Xeon and I are climbing from the rubble when we see Cohen and Borman talking next to the helicopter. They start walking toward us the minute we clear the dirt.

Xeon is smiling, knowing her instincts once again paid off.

I look at her and nod. "Nice work, Xeon. You're shaping up to be a first rate soldier."

She punches me in the arm.

"I take that back. You are a first rate soldier. It's me who's shaping up...to appreciate your instincts."

"Thanks, Lucky."

"Find anything?" Cohen shouts, half way to where we are.

I nod, but wait until we get closer to start diving in. I scan the horizon—more from habit than anything, but certainly can't help but wonder if we're being watched. It would make sense.

As the four of us meet up, I turn to Xeon to let her share what we found.

"Yes, we did. Several interesting things. In fact, I'd say we hit a sort of jackpot. But I'm going to let her explain; she did the digging."

"We've been very lucky, guys," she starts, elbowing me in the ribs. "We found ledgers that leads us directly to accounts, both offshore and in our Nation's capital."

The two men look to one another and then to me.

"Exactly," I emphatically said. "All roads lead somewhere. And if I were a guessing man, Caprese has something to do with it. However, as I've said before—and you'll just have to work with me on this—I owe him.

All three nod, then Peter Cohen asks, "Speaking of, what's he up to today?"

I hesitate, scanning the perimeter again. Someone's watching us, I think.

"Stayed behind at the hotel. He's...looking into some things for me." I check my watch. "He'll call me when he's done. Then, we'll swing back, grab him and go from there."

There was an awkward silence before Xeon picked back up. "The other thing that we learned was the surprising part. Well, except to Mr. Lucky, here. He brought it up first."

"It was just a hunch," I say, not trying to make a big deal about it. "You'da come up with the same conclusion. It all started to make sense when..."

Suddenly, a flash got my attention out of the corner of my eye. I knew what it was and instinctively didn't look in the direction. Everyone sensed it, immediately on high-alert.

"DROP!" I shouted to everyone, pushing Xeon to the ground.

BANG! BANG! BANG! BANG!

The ammunition whizzed by, missing us by inches. In a split second, I knew it was a high-powered rifle. It was likely a Cheytech .308; just like mine. Another fraction of a second and we'd have been massacred in broad daylight.

We scattered, staying low to the ground; each one of us, pulling guns from our sides. Fortunately, there was enough random scattered walls from the earlier explosion to provide us cover.

Gun drawn and eyes furiously scanning the perimeter; I see nothing. Wait! I see a camouflaged Jeep tearing away. I may not know that vehicle, but I have a strong guess who's behind it.

In seconds, the four of us are in the chopper, lifted off and in hot pursuit. Xeon and I are watching out either side, as we maneuver over low mountain ranges.

"Guess they should have figured we'd be able to follow them," Peter shouts into his mic.

We look at one another and laugh.

"Maybe they wanted us to see them," I say. This gets their attention.

"There's no telling where he's leading us." Xeon says.

"No doubt," I respond.

In the next two minutes, our high-speed chase ends as the Jeep disappears into a thick forest on the outskirts of town. We can't see anything from here.

"Damn!" Peter shouts. Shaking his head, he motions for Borman to circle around.

"Lost him. But, I can hover and maybe flush..."

"Don't worry." I tap both guys on the shoulders. "We've got a good idea who sent that person, or persons, to hit us. Fortunately, they missed...IF indeed they meant to miss. Maybe they wanted us to follow them. If so, then we have a whole different story."

Xeon taps me and shakes her head, "They've gone under. We won't find them. I say we bounce."

"Agreed. If we drop now, it'll be smack dab in the middle of an ambush." I chew on that a second. "And we'd be worse off than before. Let's head back, guys. Gotta be smart and strategic...not renegade and reactionary."

"Agreed," Borman and Cohen say.

They spin us around and we're off.

23.

THE SWITCHBACK

MONDAY, MAY 3 — 1201Z

We returned to Jose Marti International Airport in Havana, within a short time. I knew we would have to get back to the hotel to get Caprese, but wasn't going to spend time worrying about that until I heard from him. I wasn't sure all that he was up to, but then, it wasn't my concern. Sometimes you have to bend the rules, in order to make them work, I thought. And these days, I found myself in the business of bending them a lot.

As the four of us made our way to the hangar, I hung back, letting Peter, Josh and Xeon get ahead. I needed a few minutes to get lost in thought. Random thoughts started bouncing around my head like a pinball machine.

Mack is still alive. I'm not sure how I know it, but I do. Donovan is alive and well and certainly planning his next move. But, what does he need with Mack? He won't make a kidnapping play. Don't think it's his style. Or, the highest and best use of his time. What would I do if I were in his place? I hadn't shared the details of the evidence we found in the safe back in Cienfuegos with our guys. We were interrupted. The ledgers, linking Donovan to allies across the country, weren't a surprise.

It was Donovan's former military background that was the surprise.

Ex-Navy. Highly respected. Something must have gone terribly wrong for him to be discharged. I needed to know why. Was there a link? Were his guys ex-military too? Some of them seemed like it, while others didn't.

Gitmo! Where'd that come from? Who knows, but every time something comes from nowhere, it usually means something. What was it?

I needed to check in on Randall and Tony, but Mack was priority one. I would make it a point to...

Wait! Concentrate on the branches of service. Randall was a Marine, as was Tony. I was Army—Special Forces. Mack was Navy—a Seal. And Donovan was Navy. Was he a Seal? Was there a connection?

As the others were making their way to the hangar, Xeon stopped and was watching me.

"You coming?" she shouted.

Nodding, I joined her and we made our way to the hangar.

"You were mighty deep in thought."

"Yeah, I guess," I reply. "Ever had something scratch at the back of your head but you couldn't quite find its meaning?

"Uh, only like all the time. Isn't that what they call occupational hazard?" She smiles. And she's right; it is.

Peter met us at the door and handed both of us new cellphones. They had special encryption capabilities, along with all the other latest tricks. We referred to the arsenal they arrived with as coming from DC's Toy Closet. Think: James Bond, but less gimmicky.

Xeon's cellphone rings within seconds.

"Xeon," she answered. "Yes. This is me," she continued, providing a host of details to confirm her identity.

Then my phone rings. I expected the same. Answering it, I answer, "Lucky."

"It's about time you got a new phone...Lucky." The voice on the line was familiar, but because of the loud noise outside the hangar, I was having a hard time deciphering."

"Tony?" I was shocked. The doctors had told us there was less than a fifty-fifty chance that he would live.

"Damn straight, Lucky," he coughed. "Back from the dead."

"Man, it's good to hear your voice. Doc said you weren't..."

"Yeah, yeah, Likely wasn't gonna make it," he replied, coughing again, but picking up enthusiasm in his tone. "Then again, you know me. Tough to keep a hard man down, right?"

"You bet. How ya feeling, anyway? And how's Pops?"

"I'm good. Gonna take a bit to bounce back, but I'm up for the fight. Randall? He's good. He's across the room getting his nails done as we speak." He laughs.

I could hear Randall yelling across the room. I heard something along the lines of Weenie and Woosie. I could tell they were going to be alright. Thank you God, I caught myself thinking.

"Hey, Carter, anything new with Mack? I wish I could be there to..."

"Dude," I interrupt, "Stop. You will. Soon enough. And no—no word...yet."

He could tell by my voice that I was confident we would

find him. Just as we had found him and Randall.

We chat a few more minutes and I was about to let him go and ring off, when the word Gitmo came to mind again. I couldn't suppress it any longer, knowing that sometimes—often in fact, those pings were where the answers lived.

Xeon, Peter and Josh were clowning around across the deck. And even in their clowning around, I knew they had my back. I was certain how Xeon was wired—just like her father. I had a good feeling about Josh, given he was one of us. And my instincts were the same for Peter, as he was a retired version of us. I knew they were just waiting for their next order. And I was the one to give it to them. I watched in admiration because I knew each of them were willing to lie down their lives for Mack. That was a powerful bond that few people in the world felt. Soldiers knew that feeling of belonging, but few others did.

"Tony, before you go, I gotta ask you something."

"Shoot."

"I've been simmering about something. It has to do with our group being from several forces...what I mean is, we're all brothers, but we're also..."

"Cut to it, Carter," Tony said abruptly. He didn't like to see anyone waffle—the least of which, me.

"What I'm getting to is...Donovan is, or rather was—one of us." I waited a beat. "Navy."

The silence on the other end of the line was deafening. I know Tony; he needs a moment to process something like that.

"What. The. Hell?" he said, the vibrancy returning to his voice.

"Yeah, when Xeon and I went to examine the remains of

the power plant, we discovered a safe. There were enough transactional records that could be easily traced and translated to put that bastard away for a long time."

"Hmm."

"Not only that, there were other documents. Classified. They showed more than enough evidence for..."

"Dishonorable discharge," he interrupts. "Saw that coming."

"Copy that."

"Shit."

"Yep."

"Guess that makes some sort of sense," he adds. "But what's the..."

"Assaulting an officer. While under the influence."

"Geez."

"It gets worse," I hesitate. "He pistol-whipped an O2."

"Damn. The idiot have some kind of death wish?"

"No doubt."

"What was..."

"Petty Officer, Second Class."

"An E5 hitting an O2? The balls on that steer, son."

"Now, you see...Well, it makes better sense for me now."

"His stature. His timing..." he hesitates.

I let him keep putting it together.

"I watched the way he led his men. It was his method. The way they admired, maybe even feared him."

"Exactly," I say.

"Bet you his recruits were all..."

"Fallouts," we both say at the same time.

Fallouts were what we called men who couldn't take the heat. Either they had one of a variety of chemical addictions, were dysfunctional—as in they had some mental incompatibility with the Corp, or they just didn't like taking orders. Whatever it was, they either just fell out, or were made to fall out.

I hear Randall shouting something across the room. "What's the old man saying?"

"Hold on. Let him tell you." He whispers, "Old bird's driving me bananas."

"I'll get you out of there, just give me..."

"Give you what?" Randall barks. Evidently, he grabbed the phone from Tony.

"Yeah, tell Tony goodbye for me. I gotta bounce. Sir!"

"Just a god-damned minute, son. Aren't you going to ask how your old man's doing?"

"I did. You just told me."

"Huh?"

"By being a bulldog. Do you have to boss everyone around?"

I didn't give him the opportunity to answer, before I add, "Anyhow, I'm glad you're better."

"I'm 95% son. What I want to know is..."

He stops. This is something he often did: hesitate for effect. It was his way of saying Wait for it.

"Go on," I say, begrudgingly.

"Why in the hell-fire missile haven't you found Mack, yet?"

The last 24 hours have been a blur, Mack thought to himself. I can't tell if I'm coming or going. Intense hunger washed over him like nausea. Pain coursed through his wrists and ankles like razor blades. And blindness was the thing that terrified him most. He had lost the vision in one eye, but he couldn't tell about the other, as he had been blindfolded immediately before being tossed into a helicopter. He assumed it was one of Donovan's. He couldn't be sure. The last two things he remembered was having a needle being shoved into his thigh. The hot, numbing liquid surged through his body, thanks in part to an overactive shot of adrenaline now coursing through his veins. That happened the minute a deafening blast had exploded nearby their transport. The other thing he recalled was the pungent odor of something burning. It could have been gasoline, or oil, or metal and timber, for all he knew. The engine didn't sound right, too.

Last thing I expected was to end up on this side of the dirt, he thought, becoming more coherent by the second.

He heard muffled voices in the distance. Again, he assumed they belonged to Donovan and his team. He tried to move, but couldn't—either because of constraints, or drugs that filled his enormous frame.

All I have to do is remain calm. And listen. At least my hearing will help, he thought. Listen closely.

Carter sat there listening to his father. He admired Randall for everything he'd had taught him, but there were times Carter just wanted to cold-cock his old man.

"I'm doing everything I can. I'm working with Caprese and..."

"You're WHAT?" Randall barked.

His energy had evidently returned, given the volume of that inquiry. I tried to keep my cool. This was simply Randall's way: bark first, ask questions later. Or, in this case, make the bark and the question one in the same. Tony understood what I was doing. My team of Xeon, Peter and Josh knew what I was doing. I knew what I was trying to do. And while we didn't have all the answers, we certainly had a good deal more than what Randall

"Bulldog" Matheson was providing. I let the air grow quiet before returning the volley.

"Caprese saved my life." I hesitate, then add, "Sir."

The tension is palpable.

I continue.

"He saved the life of my team. And as you watched, he saved your and Tony's lives. So, I'd say the fair thing is to play ball...at least until we learn otherwise."

After a good ninety seconds of silence, he spoke, "My apologies, Carter. You're right. I hope you'll forgive me."

I nearly fell from my chair. I've known my father for decades, and that was easily the first time he'd ever spoken those two, albeit short, sentences—in my life.

"Understood. No apologies needed," I quietly reply, and while not completely agreeing with the statement, felt it was best to let it go for now.

"What can Tony and I do to help...son?"

That's exactly what I needed right now: a complete team effort with one of the most important men in my life...to help me find the other most important man in my life.

Mack knew that if he played along with Donovan one of two things would likely happen: either Donovan would appreciate Mack's willingness to work with him, and may show some leniency as to how he would handle Mack. Or, if he stood up to him—as was his Standard Operating Procedure, he wouldn't take any shit, but at the very least, would work to make some breaks come together.

That may work. At the end of the day, Mack was not going to roll over and play dead, no matter who the scumbags were controlling the remote control of this life. Furthermore, he and Carter both knew that there was a zero's chance in hell of Mack giving anyone anything, in the way of Intel. That was a 100% impossibility. End of story.

So, Mack laid there, practically starving, numb in his hands and feet because of the severe restriction of blood flow—thanks to the violent and careless way he had been bound. And, on top of it all, I'm fucking blind in one eye because one of your stupid-ass gorillas beat my face with the butt of a machine gun, he shouted in his head.

"Deep breath. Stay calm. Listen Closely," he whispered to himself, remaining fully aware of all that was happening around him. He could hear voices in the distance. One of them could have been Donovan's; he wasn't sure.

There is bound to be a point of weakness with this guy, he thinks, There always is.

Before I ring off, I ponder whether or not to mention to my father something that's been nagging at me. I have no idea what it means—if anything, but I continue to swat at it like a pesky gnat.

"Okay, son, guess we'll speak more later. Doc says I'm pretty much good to go inside the next 24 hours. Tony, on the other hand, while able to get up and around, won't be back to normal for another couple of weeks. Best news was when Doc told him he'd be able to keep the foot. He's lost most of the feeling in it—which won't likely return, but at least he won't be walking with a plastic peg."

I can hear Tony laughing in the background. He's a good sport.

"Hey, Pops. Can I run something past you?"

"Sure thing. Shoot."

"It's about Gitmo. I was wondering if you knew anything about what's going on there these days. And if you think there's either any connection to this Donovan lunatic..."

I was beginning to feel self-conscious and I wasn't sure why, but continue, "Maybe he has some wacky connection to it. Am I crazy?"

Gitmo, or Guantanamo Bay, is a United States military prison, or detention camp located within Guantanamo Bay Naval Base in Cuba. It was established in 2002 when Secretary of Defense Rumsfeld said the camp would be established to detain extraordinarily dangerous people. Here, detainees would be interrogated and prosecuted for war crimes. The camp had entertained any number of considerations; they included closing the camp because of abusive torture that was alleged to have taken place, as well as a Congress who wanted to keep it open instead of relocating prisoners to the United States for trial or detention.

There was a long silence on the phone.

"Yes, son; you're crazy, but that's besides the point."

It provided just a bit of levity to an otherwise stressful interchange.

"Let's just say there are those among us who have supported the use of Gitmo for a number of reasons. Not that I have to tell you, son, but there are many people out there who want to bring grave harm to our country."

"Yes, Sir."

"And I, for one, believe that it's a good thing. Frankly, it allows us have a place to take the loonies and...well, handle them the way they need to be handled. And all within the confines of what's right—in order to get the answers we need."

"Do you think there's any connection between Donovan and Gitmo?"

"Interesting. Well, it is a Naval Air Base. There's that

connection."

I stop.

"Wait, did I tell you...that he was Navy?"

"Tony did. Well, I heard it on the line when you were telling Tony."

My dad always had a way of getting information without my knowing it. Then again, I suppose that's what took him to the top of the ranks.

"Fair enough. I would have told you..."

"Carter, it's fine. I know you two have a connection we don't. No big. I just want to find the cocksucker who took our man, and then take him apart, piece by piece."

"Yes, Sir. We will. I'm on it. In fact, I told Tony..."

"I heard. Count on us for whatever you need. Anything."

"Thank you. I have to run. I'll be back in touch shortly."

I rang off and start putting the last few details together—some of them made sense; others didn't. Not all of it had to. I just need to get a few pieces started, and I knew exactly where to begin. My team and I would fly to Gitmo Bay. It's only about ninety minutes in the Apache, but I had a feeling something would turn up that would help me know the whereabouts of my pal.

I shout to Peter and Xeon who are drinking coffee. "Let's fall out. I know where we need to head next!"

Mack had fallen asleep. No doubt, fatigue had gotten the better of him. Even in this state, he felt something oddly familiar with his surroundings. He wasn't sure if it was the smell, the noises, or what. As he became more clear-headed, he realized his mouth had been taped closed.

What, they don't want me to scream? What would I say anyway?

He laid there wondering what would happen next.

Carter is on his way, he thought. If there's anything I know about him, it's that he won't stop until he finds me. It's just the way he's wired.

Keeping the faith, is all Mack could think about. Well, that and staying alive. Suddenly, a noise in the distance got his attention. It was a familiar voice.

Was that…is that…Carter?

24.

THE RENEGOTIATION

MONDAY, MAY 3 — 1351Z

Inside the past 24 hours or more, a man named Donovan was on a mission. He quickly assessed the situation and soon realized it had reached a melting point. Moreover, he saw Carter and his crew were more than he had bargained for.

Carter had seen that same happen several times inside the past week. It had become painfully obvious that Carter's team was not to be taken lightly. And even with all the military training Donovan had, along with the strength of his men—most of whom were recruits of one sort or another, they weren't nearly the match for his opponent.

Donovan Blair had been in precarious places before. You didn't get where he was without running into a fair share of dangerously difficult situations. He was used to pushing people aside—either by manipulation, torture, or death. Sometimes by all three. Donovan was accustomed to pushing boundaries, stepping on people on the way up the ladder, and even to the point of catapulting people, similar to his own caliber, to the breaking point. It was what got him dismissed from the Navy. Donovan was the quintessential example of being at the wrong place at the wrong time and pushing the wrong man to the wrong limits.

Donovan, aka Scorpion, recalled sensing the poisonous venom of the scorpion that bit him. The first time.

He and several of his mates were stationed off the coast of Israel, due west of Haifa, a town that sat halfway between Gaza and Beirut, Lebanon. They were part of the initiation of the Iraqi "no-fly zone." The NFZ had been set into motion by the United States, United Kingdom and France after the Gulf War to protect the Kurds in northern Iraq and Shite Muslims in the south. The purpose: to keep the Iraqi aircraft from flying inside the zones.

During his tour of duty, Donovan would be stationed on both aircraft carriers and aboard submarines. He preferred the open-air to the under-water vessel. On this particular mission, the submersible mode of transportation had been chosen by the powers above. What he never shared with either the recruiting administrator, the future Commanding Officer, or even the pals with whom he bunked, was a secret that was not only difficult to keep quiet, but one that would eventually push him to the absolute limit of sanity.

Not only was Donovan afraid of the dark, but he was also claustrophobic. So, during a different mission operating in the Mediterranean—in the middle of the night, and aboard the USS Pittsburgh—a sub that was carrying Tomahawk Land Attack Missiles, an entirely different shit storm went down. It wasn't unusual for men to be deployed for months on end. Furthermore, they were prone to becoming a bit distraught—aka cabin crazy, during those tightly enclosed times. On one such evening, while playing poker in the belly of the beast, one of the men going up against Donovan pulled out a scorpion to taunt his opponents. Such things were completely illegal, and everyone knew it. When this wisecracker went to toss his scorpion at Donovan, after accusing him of cheating, Donovan did what any red-blooded American would do: defend his honor. And he did that by stomping on the scorpion. It was instantly killed. What Donovan didn't know was that it was an extremely rare scorpion called a deathstalker. Not only were they expensive, because of the rarity, but they were extremely dangerous. They truly were killers. That same night, and after way too many drinks, he paid a visit to his competitor. However, in transit to the cabin, a soldier, one visiting Lieutenant Junior Grade, Mark Kominsky, rounded a corner, and expecting a salute was instead met with a pummeling to the face—of one very drunk Petty Officer Donovan Blair.

Former Petty Officer Blair was dishonorably discharged for reckless endangerment, being intoxicated while on duty, and the worse of all, assault with a weapon. He beat LTJG Kominsky nearly to death with the butt of his 9mm. On his discharge papers, he got the offense written up as "mentally unfit" by the Navy. What others would learn later was that he suffered bi-polar tendencies, complicated by bouts of schizophrenia and manic depression. By many, he was referred to as "nut job." Shortly thereafter, he adopted the nickname of Scorpion, as he began running a clandestine world by his own rules, diving deep into the world of narcotics and gun sales. He quickly adopted the deadly arachnid as a killing device masquerading as a pet.

Donovan sipped black coffee, staring into the distance while struggling to put the pieces together. He desperately wanted to come to terms with one fact: How could he be booted from the one organization he wanted to belong to more than anything else? Moreover, how could he rid himself of his demons? And do so in the most obscure way possible.

Dammit, he thinks. Just when I was getting what I wanted and where I wanted it, these clowns have to get in my way and ruin everything.

Donovan sat motionless, trying to recall how many months and how much money he had spent retrofitting the power plant of nuclear and cold fusion into a powerful plant of narcotics and cash infusion. Fortunately, the Scorpion had a plan of setting a trap for incoming violators by setting the plant tunnels to blow in case any authorities were to confiscate any drugs or personal information.

What am I going to do now, Donovan thought, referring to a business where he'd lost millions of dollars in drugs in the blink of an eye. And what should I do with the collateral I hold against Carter.

"What if I trade Mack for Carter, and take Carter down once and for all," he mumbled.

That'd certainly rid me of many problems, he thought, quickly coming to the conclusion that Caprese had turned out to be a bag of useless hot air.

"Plus, it'd be a nice payback for losing all my shit!" Donovan shouted to no one in particular.

The simple fact was that none of his men were paying him any attention. Instead, they stood nearby joking among themselves, polishing their guns and packing their bags.

It was smart to come back here. It'd be the last place they'd think to look, he thought.

Looking across the vast hangar, his eyes fell on the trunk that held some of the precious cargo he'd been able to save during their recent maneuver off the coast of the nuclear power plant.

Right under their noses, the scorpion smiled.

Given that Mack had been zip-tied, gagged and bound in a way he couldn't quite figure out, he was disoriented and out of his element.

I'm scared. This is crazy. I can't get...myself...out of this fix. Am I in the trunk of a car...a shipping crate? Keep your cool...we'll get out of this.

Bang, Bang...Bang!

Randall and Tony sat in their hospital room quietly, one stared out the window—the other, stared at the ceiling. It felt like an eternity, before Tony spoke.

"Boss, something tells me Carter's going to head to Gitmo to dig around."

"Yeah."

"It's a loss leader, ya know."

"Why do you say that?"

"I don't know."

One thing Randall knew about Tony was that he'd always had feelings about things. And eight out of ten times, Tony was right. Not sorta right, but spot on right. That's why Randall took the time to listen and get Tony to talking more.

"Tell me your thoughts, pal."

Tony had been lying completely still staring at the ceiling, since hanging up with Carter. His eyes seemed to see through the ceiling, as though watching something happen miles above them.

“Well, first of all, we both know that our beloved government set that place up in order to get to the bottom of the very best of kept secrets. It was really all about torturing and killing, if need be, to get the Intel we needed. And we all like that idea. Agreed?”

“Of course,” Randall said quietly.

“If you’ll recall, the Department of Defense, were the dudes that first had the bright idea to keep it all secret—the identity of the pricks being held, that is. But after the suits lost attempts to defy the beloved Freedom of Information Act request from—of all people, the Associated Press. It wasn’t until after that push that some loudmouth would release the fact we…they…were holding nearly 800 men and boys in the camp.”

Tony shifts his eyes from the ceiling to Randall for the first time in twenty minutes. Randall feels the look, but doesn’t distract from the moment by looking at him. Instead, he simply grunts. Tony grins and resumes the story.

“Okay, I see I have you riveted. So, you’ll recall when Bush political appointees at the U. S. Office of Legal Counsel, Department of Justice advised the Bush suits that Gitmo should be considered outside U. S. legal jurisdiction.”

“Uh huh.”

“Bush went on to assert—right, or otherwise, that detainees were not entitled to any of the protections of the Geneva Conventions. So, fast forward a few years later to when detainees were entitled to minimal protections listed under Common Article 3 of the Geneva

Conventions. And a month later…"

"Wait," Randall interrupted, "What are you a walking law book? Better yet, how do you…"

"Shut it. I'm not done yet. And for the record, I read. A lot. Usually when you're out chasing bad guys—or the next wife…and leave me to wash and wax the Bell Ranger." He waited. Randall said nothing.

"Like I was saying…so about a month later, the DOD issued a memo saying detainees would, in the future, be entitled to protection under that same Article 3. Now, as we both know, there isn't any abuse or torture…"

Randall laughed and Black joined him.

"Damn, that's funny. Okay, I know you'll be glad I'm almost done. So, now you have those pacifists who cry Protection and Civility and Humanity and whatever else," Tony mockingly whined. "Yet, these same pussies are the people who want to save our country from destruction by the bad guys. So they say—they, being Amnesty International, that Gitmo is the, 'Gulag of our times.' Of course it is, you pathetic left-wing liberal nut cakes."

"Your point?" Randall sighed. "Please?"

"Just that America wants US to keep them safe. America wants the BAD GUYS to be done away with, so we can run along in our over-sized SUVs, eating out at over-sized buffet counters, while taking over-sized vacations wherever the hell we want to…while remaining protected from all the evil in the world…but when it comes time to FINDING those assholes who live and die trying to make sure those of us living in the U-S-of-A die in our tracks…"

He stopped.

Silence.

"And?" Randall asked.

"Screw it. They want our lives to be indispensable so their lives can be protected, yet when we put it ALL on the line to FIND the SECRETS that will PROTECT us all...and we'll do it BY ANY MEANS POSSIBLE...then they cry, 'Don't hurt them. They have freedoms too."

Again, more silence.

"It's bullshit," Tony said so quietly he can barely be heard, but Randall knew what he said.

"It is, Tony. It most certainly is."

"Reason for that long tale around the barn is to try and see where things really are in comparison to where Carter thinks Donovan may be. My gut says Carter may think Donovan has a plant in Gitmo—perhaps using some of the rejects from there to help work the factory. Better yet, since Gitmo is dark in many ways, there may be additional funding coming out of there without the eyes of democracy on him. Not to mention, Donovan has ties to the underground. Why do you think they call Cuba The Devil's Playground?

"So, what the fuck we gonna do?"

"What do you think..." Randall asked, then before he can finish his question, Tony is sitting on the side of his bed, trying to slide a pant leg over his heavily bandaged foot.

"Whoa, whoa, whoa..." Randall said, getting up from his recliner, steadying himself, then trying to maneuver across the room to stop Tony.

Tony watched him teeter and still continued to dress.

"C'mon, Gramps. Let's get your walker," Tony laughed, now nearly fully dressed and grabbing a bag of personal items from the small closet. "Don't know about you, but I'm not going to lie around here and hope someone will protect my freedoms while I watch some daytime soaps that I can't understand—knowing one of our men is out there hopefully still alive...and wondering WHERE ARE THEY!"

Tony is out the door and down the hall, by the time Randall had finished gathering his things. He looks to the corner where there's parked two walkers and a cane.

"No way," Randall mumbled, pushing the door behind him.

The two men left behind, excluding Donovan, are called Numbers and Pony. Numbers was the brainiac and nervous one. He was always tossing something like a tennis ball around. Nervous energy, he called it. He continued to bounce a handball against the wall, nearby boxes and storage containers. With nine soldiers down and only three to go, plus the woman—a late-comer to the party, the dwindling crew, wasn't quite the nasty dozen they were before.

Donovan was feeling weaker than before, when his entire team numbered twelve. This made his manic tendencies to become worse. He crossesd the vast closed hangar, watching his men as they watched him. He enjoyed the fear he instilled in people like them. He slung the HK over his shoulder and adjusted his belt, securing his Glock in its holster. He glared at both man, thinking, You're weak...And you're weak. When his eyes came to rest on his girl-toy, Mo-Wang, he stopped and stared.

Should I keep her around, or let her go. She's smart, but maybe she wants to steal my money, he thinks.

"What's the latest with our prisoner?" he asked.

"Well, I doubt that he's very comfortable, but he's certainly not going anywhere," she said. An evil grin creases her porcelain skin.

"Good. In both regards," he replied, eyeballing his watch, his men and the cargo. He walked to a window and scanned the horizon then the tarmac. Looking left then right, he didn't see much activity.

Just then, Carter and his team exit his neighbor's hangar.

Must have fallen for the diversion I left behind, he mumbled.

"What's that?" MoWang asked.

Distracted, he replied, "Nothing. Guessing he's headed to the hospital to check on his old man."

Disregarding his slightly unbalanced energy today, she ran a checklist for him. "The chopper is prepped and ready to fly. We've got plenty of ammo on board. The boat and sub contacted me less than fifteen minutes ago; both are ready to rendezvous when you give the word."

"Good," he replied. "Pony, Numbers, it's left to the four of us. Hate that we've lost all those good men, but often that's what it takes to gain our freedom. And to do what we want to do."

Both men nod in agreement.

That's right boys, nod like the good little sheep that you are, he thought.

"Okay, we have less than seven hours to be ready. In that time, we need to do three things and three things only. Are you listening?"

They nod, adding "Yes, Sir," for affect.

"Good. First, my instinct tells me Carter and his men will head to the hospital to check on his father and his buddy. Then, they'll either head back to Cienfuegos to see if there's anything they missed. Which they won't. Or...they'll do something ridiculous like head to Gitmo to see if they can learn anything from my contacts. Which they won't. Why? Because none of my people will snitch. Which means they'll head back here. If they don't, then we'll dispose of Mack on the way to the Keys. If he does show up, then I'll bargain one for the other.

"What do you mean exactly?" MoWang asked.

Are you stupid, he thought, but instead said, "Excellent question. What I mean is that I will allow Mack to live IF Carter turns himself over to me. Which is what he will do. He will have to save his pal's life. He's hard-headed. And I'll play along, as the last nice thing I do."

His team looked at him, expressionless.

"If it doesn't work," he continued, "I'll just kill Mack anyway. And if I need to kill Carter—which I will do eventually, then I can kill two birds with one stone."

Donovan chuckled, "Or one gun, as the case may be."

MoWang stared as him, not sure if he's stable or not. The other two men are pretty sure he isn't. "Either way, we're out of here and on our way to the Keys. Between the chopper, the boat and the sub, we'll have three avenues of possibility. Luckily, we had stored up the boat and the sub before the plant blew. We still have several millions of goods to sell—making us many more millions in return."

The team smiled at one another. Their ship is about to come in.

"So, let's grab some chill time and then we'll make our way out of this country."

They started to disband, when Donovan stopped them.

"Numbers, let's confirm just a few things. The boat has been loaded with drugs in the hull and fish atop, right?"

"Yes, sir. We grabbed a large fishing boat and stocked it accordingly," he smiles. "Two of our local fishermen will make easy work out of that. They'll be departing from

Carbonara, just due East of Matanzas. We put up our two policeman friends at the Blau Marina Varadero Resort—along with a couple girls for the night. They were very happy to comply. They'll rendezvous at Carbonara, thanks to one of our city crew there."

"Good. And the midget-sub?" Donovan asked.

He nodded, "The 865 Piranha was delivered and offloaded in the Bahamas, thanks to our Russian friends. It's an awesome vessel, sir. It's all titanium, super quiet and has plenty of heat on board, just in case things get out of hand.

"Nice. And the rendezvous times..."

"They're due to meet us in the Florida Straits, halfway to the Keys," he said, "They're carrying all the hardware we'll need for Miami."

"Excellent. All coming together nicely. Mo and I will get there ahead of time and be sure our channels are all wide open. There shouldn't be any problem. We have all the regular points covered and once we land, we'll split things along the waterways and meet up in Miami. Then, inside the next day or two, we can start Phase 2 of Scorpion Strike."

25.

THE SETUP

MONDAY, MAY 3 — 1659Z

Randall and Tony looked about as good as two old guys who'd been run hard and put up wet could look. One had been stung by a scorpion and lived to tell about it. The other was shot in the foot and was able to walk again. Both had been kidnapped and tortured for hours on end. Plus, the two of them had been nearly starved to death in the process. With dozens of tours of duty under their belts, numbers of wives under their care, and one too many drinks due them the minute they get out of this pickle, all in all, the two men knew what it meant to serve their country. It took more than military training, or a formal education. It took more than guts and stamina. It took pride in their country, and in what they were called to do with their lives.

They'd escaped the hospital, commandeered a taxi to get them back to the Havana airport, and were on target to arrive the same time Carter would. Both men hoped to get there before Carter left for Gitmo.

“Do you really think Carter feels that Gitmo is a good use of time in trying to find his pal,” Tony asks.

“Course not. I just think he feels his time has run out; his options are gone. And frankly, I don't blame him. Carter's running this whole freakin' campaign, nearly single-handedly.”

“Hey, now wait just a minute,” Tony interrupted. “I think we've done...”

“Settle down, Nancy. Keep your skirt on. I mean in the big picture; it's all been up to him. Look, we got hood-winked by Caprese trying to get out of Nicaragua. That left us in a pickle. I still don't know how he managed that, or how Carter was able to find us. Nonetheless, he did, and here we are.”

“Well, not in all that great condition,” Tony said, lighting a cigar with a butane torch.

“I think...” Randall started. “Where'd you get that?”

“Uh, we're in Cuba, Randall. Where do you think I got it,” Tony replied, reaching in his pocket. “I mean them.” He handed Randall one.

“Thanks. You're a champ,” he added, biting the tip off the dark, fat cigar. “Hand me that...”

Tony handed him the torch, blowing thick blue smoke in Randall's face, then swatting it away, laughing.

The cab driver found it funny, as well.

“Funny. Anyhow, as I was saying, Mr. ADHD...”

“Really?”

Randall ignored him and started again, “Bottom line is this: Carter will find Mack. He always has and always will. What worries me, though, is that either he, or we run into

Donovan—aka Scorpion Sucker, in the process."

"Just wait until I get my hands on him. I'll take that 9-mil and shove it so far up his ass, then pull the trigger, he'll be reading the paper from the top of his head." He sucked hard on his cigar and blew it out the window, pulling bits of tobacco from his lips at the same time.

"That's a visual, Tony."

"Yeah. Thought you'd like that."

My company and I left Cienfuegos and started to head to Gitmo. We thought, or rather, I thought that it may be a good idea. But after much discussion with my teammates, the idea was tossed out and we were now headed back to Havana. We'd land at the airport, grab Peter's Jeep, and drive to the hospital to check on Randall and Tony.

"On the off-chance those two girls have escaped Nurse Ratchet's grip," I say, "I'll have to assume that they'll be making their way back to the airport. Probably expecting me to be there."

"Sounds like a plan, Lucky," Xeon says. "And a much better one than heading all the way down to Gitmo just to find out what they say is true."

She left that alone, knowing it would only stir up a hornet's nest and make me cranky. And given I hadn't had much food, rest, or sex in a good many days, she felt confident I wouldn't take it well. She also knew there was a good chance I'd toss some shit in her direction. Xeon had neither the time nor the patience to put up with either.

"You think there's any chance that Donovan's gone back to the power plant?" Peter asks. "You know, to see if we're there...or we left anything behind, or..."

I shake my head. "No way in hell." There's nothing there he needs. Well, besides the papers in the safe—but you can be sure he has duplicates of all that stuff."

"What about the millions in drugs," Xeon asks.

"My guess? Drop in the bucket, babe. I mean, this guy's smart—a genuine maniac, but remember: he was one of us. So, he's had the training to think this through. Thoroughly. Moreover, he's been printing pills and growing grass for a super long time. I'm 100% positive he's got plenty more where that came from. No doubt in my mind."

All three nod in agreement. They knew it was the smart play.

I check the time. It was getting late. I had no idea where Donovan would have tried to hide Mack. I smack Xeon's arm, motioning for her duffle bag. "Xeon, toss me your bag. I want to look at the maps again."

"Geez, you and maps. You own stock in Google?" She replies, handing me a stack of maps.

"Huh? Yeah, sure. Lots of it," I dismiss her, looking at the country of Cuba.

It's not that big. There's plenty of access all around us. I scan the major cities and towns. There are plenty of small airports dotting the whole...

I stop. Wait...I keep thinking...

"Hey Peter," I bark, punching him on the arm, startling him in the process. There's one large abandoned plant in this country, right?"

"Ha! No way. There are dozens. Think about it, historically speaking, what with the Communist regime, Castro..."

"Yeah, yeah, right, right," I interrupt. "Okay, but there are few ports—you know, whereby..."

"Lots, Lucky. Plenty," he now interrupts.

"Alright. Copy that. But look," I say, pointing at the

map—my finger scanning all across the maps. "There are tons of airports. With nobody thinking anything about Apache's or Bell Rangers or the like, coming and going."

"Yeah. True," he says.

"Xeon, what are you getting at, Carter?"

"He would want us to believe that he would be heading to any number of places besides another airport."

Xeon shakes her head.

"And you know he's getting the heck out of Dodge. That's the business he's in."

Peter chimes in, "Yes. Makes total sense."

"So…if I'm the maniac drug dealer that…"

My phone rings. I check the screen. Looks familiar. I answer.

"Carter?"

"Yeah, Caprese. What's up? What'd you find?"

"A lot. Let's just say, it's a good idea to get back to Havana as soon as you can."

"We're on our way now. Where should we…"

"Meet me back at the airport. I'm heading over to the hospital to get your dad and Tony, but meet me at the airport!"

"Copy that. See you in…" I look to Josh and Peter, they both hold up five fingers. "We'll be there in less than 5 minutes."

We both ring off. Suddenly, I feel like I best get ready for what feels like some sort of showdown on Main Street.

26.

THE SHOWDOWN

MONDAY, MAY 3 — 1703Z

My team had just enough time to catch their breath, when we hovered over the helipad of Jose Marti International Airport. This was the place it all started. As we were landing, I spotted Donovan's Black SUV pull out from the neighboring hangar.

"What the hell?" I shout. My mind was racing.

"What is he doing back here?" Peter shouts.

"Of course," Xeon says, shaking her head.

"Yep. Just as we thought. He'd expect us to go elsewhere and spend all our time and last resources chasing a dead end. This way..."

My eyes race to look for his chopper. Nothing. Where's Mack? I thought. THINK!

Peter spoke on our headsets, "Okay, we're landing over on that side, away from where we usually land. It will give us better egress in case..."

BANG! BANG!

Two shots were fired from the SUV. Someone was wasting no time in trying to drop us like a dead bird.

"Peter, Josh, pull us outta here!" I shout.

At the same time, that's exactly what they were doing.

I spun around in my seat to see the hangar doors being pulled back and a tractor pulling the Apache from the side bay.

"Over there. That's Donovan's chopper," I shout, overstating the obvious. The adrenaline was surging through my body.

"I think we've been hit in the tail," Peter shouts.

We all look out all windows trying to see the damage. Sure enough, we had been hit. It was a graze, but that graze obviously hit some line, as there was smoke pouring out.

"I've got to set this girl down. Otherwise, we'll drop like a rock," Josh shouts, grabbing the controls and spinning us up and around—dodging any incoming bullets.

Perfect timing.

BANG! SWOOSH! BANG! SWOOSH!

Both shots miss us within inches, and Peter and Josh would have us down in a hot second. Just as we were rounding the building, I saw one of Donovan's men rolling a large container. It looks like a mini-storage box, or an oversized trunk. It had a tank attached to the top.

"MACK!" I shout, turning to Xeon, "He's in that box. Look!"

I point to the men as they head to Donovan's helicopter.

"Drop this now!" I shout, reaching for and rechecking my gun.

"Xeon, load up. The instant we touch down..."

"Like now!" Peter shouts from the front.

"You head around that way," I point, "I'll circle the other. We've got to get to that box before they reach the chopper. Drop anyone or anything inside 200 yards."

"Copy that!" Xeon shouts.

"And Peter, do me a favor..." My mind races, as I calculate the next move.

"Forget the tail, I'm begging you; lift back up and do anything you can to keep that bird from flying. We should be able to drop all the personnel, but just in case..."

"Get the hell out of here, Carter!" he shouts, pushing me out the door. Turning to Josh, he yells, "And you too, Josh."

"No way!"

"That's an order, soldier."

"Yeah? Fuck that. Sir!"

With no time to argue, they lift back up in an instant, barely closing the doors in time.

Within seconds, Xeon and I had surround the two remaining soldiers; one was pulling the chopper out from the hangar, while the other was pushing the oversized cart toward to the chopper.

Evidently, the puller was so intent on being sure the oversized helicopter wouldn't snap the wings off, he didn't even see Xeon come from behind and twist his head, snapping his spine in the process. He probably didn't feel a thing.

I, on the other hand, didn't have as much success. As I was running toward the pusher, who was trying to maneuver the cart, he spun around and pulled his gun, firing it and catching the top of my shoulder. BANG!

The bad news was that I knew in an instant that shot was going to affect my throwing arm for some time, but the good news was that it automatically threw me into a spin, allowing me to hit the ground and pump three shots into him before he hit the ground.

TAP, TAP...TAP. Left of the heart, right of the heart, and in between the eyes. His heart stopped beating before he hit the ground.

Waving Xeon to chase the helicopter, I ran to the cart that was rolling toward the tarmac. I was able to stop the roll and reached to unlock it. Unfortunately, what looked to be an oxygen tank had been ripped off the top of it, during all the ruckus.

I couldn't shake the lock, so I simply shot it. I missed the first time, but hit the second, blowing it to bits and allowing me to open the lid.

There, balled up like a little child, was my best pal. Mack's wrists and ankles were zip-tied together. He was gagged and blindfolded, but the saving grace was that he had a respirator-type oxygen mask strapped to his head. I quickly snap the ties and remove the gag and blindfold.

I help him climb out of the box. It took several minutes for him to orient himself. There was no telling how long he had been in there.

"Geez, Lucky, I was already blind...now I think I'm deaf!"

We laugh and I ask, "But you're okay, right?"

He said "What? Seriously, I can't hear you."

My heart sank.

He starts laughing.

He got me.

I'd never been so happy to see anyone in my life.

Mack was finally standing upright and on his own for the first time in days. He kept rubbing his one eye; likely trying to will it to see. I suppose only time and medical attention will provide the answers he needed.

While I was trying to catch my breath, as Xeon worked to stop the bleeding of my shoulder, Caprese pulls up at the same time as Randall and Tony. The timing was a bit uncanny.

As for Donovan, I guess I'd hesitated just enough for him to get away. My hunch was his sleek girlfriend was the pilot who got him out in the nick of time. It figures; beauty and brains behind the maniacal mind of a soldier gone rogue. The bottom line, or adjacent bottom line, was that we permanently erased his last two men.

Given that we had been keeping score of the Nasty Thirteen from the beginning, we now knew that the tally was twelve down and only one to go.

Like a scene from a movie, we saddle up, driving into the sunset to enjoy some Cuban sandwiches and entirely too many rum drinks. Sometime later, we load our choppers and make our way back to the place where we could sink our toes into the Land Of The Free and Home Of The Brave.

As for The Scorpion, he may be rich and powerful, but I'm rich with the power of a team that takes great pleasure in kicking anyone's ass who messes with the security of our great nation. Sure, there's evil in the world, and Donovan, and many like him will continually spread destruction every day, but my crew and I will do everything in our power to stop them.

I know our paths will cross again some day and when they do, Mack and I, along with a few of our friends will knuckle down and do whatever it takes to keep America safe.

27.

KNUCKLE DOWN - PROLOGUE

Donovan Blair never tired of thinking of new and inventive ways to get his products from lines of impasse to lanes of progress. He had determination and drive. He was a man of clarity and focus. And he wanted nothing more than to make money. The passion to be rich superseded everything else. It represented the quintessential element of life few people knew: Freedom. Power would be a close second. Nothing would stand in his way.

The temperature in the operating suite of his secret warehouse was low. Very low. It needed to be in order to keep the meat fresh, and the doctor wide awake. His hands were as steady as a rock. His heart rate hadn't clicked above 70 since he lifted off from Havana. But then, that was when he was running for his life. Even then, he doubted his pulse nudged 90. Donovan prided himself on his fitness. Working out every day, often for an hour or two, helped him stay fit, keep sharp and hold age at bay.

Even though Donovan was in great shape, the stress of the job immediately in front of him tested his nerves. Mo Wang, his Japanese girlfriend-assistant, wiped his brow. She caught the sweat from his forehead before it dropped to the table below, possibly contaminating his victim. He chuckled in his head at the irony of the potential of *polluting his victim.*

Nine-year old Abigail Burton was the only child of New York Mayor, Edward S. Burton. Burton was not only one of the most admired leaders in New York, but perhaps in the entire country. He had recently been commended for dramatically lowering the crime rate in Manhattan, he helped keep taxes at bay, and it was rumored he was entertaining the idea of running for President of the United States.

Donovan's team snatched Daddy's pride and joy from Central Park less than two hours ago, as Mayor Burton was hosting a televised conference on a new super train to Long Island, while Abigail's pseudo-sophisticated socialite mother was hosting a fund-raising event atop the Frick Museum on the upper-crusty East Side. Young Abigail's Nanny, french-born, Stephanie Marcheaux, was briefly distracted by a strange woman who had stopped to ask for directions by Donovan's other female assistant and second girlfriend, Margo. Margo Wheeler was proficient in six languages; French happened to be her native tongue. The orchestrated chaos occurred when Margo appeared to Abigail's nanny, hysterically crying and begging anyone to help find her little girl who had apparently wandered off.

Margo's drama helped create a handsome distraction; just enough so Abigail could be quickly escorted to a nearby black SUV. Margo and her faux husband, Ken Dawson, would escape with barely a notice by pedestrians. An adjacent 5K benefitting a random cause provided perfect additional distraction. Without a sound, she was whisked away from the unsuspecting nanny and quickly on her way to an undisclosed location in Midtown. Sean Burns, the driver, would have them out of the park and onto the West side highway in a blink.

Marcheaux looked in all directions. Abigail was gone! But so was the woman in distress and the man she assumed was the husband. Mayor Burton's employee of the past dozen years stood there frantically calling 911, worrying that she would either be fired, or buried in the Hudson River; either of which would be better than facing the possibility of being responsible for the loss of Abigail Renee Burton.

Within 22 minutes, Margo, along with Ken and Sean, Donovan's most trusted bodyguards, had the bound and sedated Abigail Burton inside a subterranean warehouse in the Chelsea district of Midtown. Donovan had chosen the Meatpacking District years ago, when meat was the currency of the day and rents were affordable enough to buy entire buildings for less than six-figures.

Donovan's concentration was admirable. Even he admired the skill with which his hands deftly opened her stomach. The razor sharp tool glistened from the bright overhead light. He stared at the angelic face of the child on the operating table, marveling at her porcelain skin and the golden hue of her soft hair. It was a sharp contrast to the bloody open cavity of her tiny torso.

Donovan worked diligently over the past two hours to open her stomach cavity, carefully slicing her from the bottom of her ribcage to lower abdomen. After removing part of her stomach, he placed several small, malleable chunks of plastic explosives inside the perfectly monitored body. The material was similar to C4, a well-known product used to drop buildings, and destroy enemies in battle. The difference between C4 and Donovan's proprietary materials; something he called K5, had the lower toxicity but higher combustible nature of the materials. Donovan took the name from an FBI training manual whereby the "kill zone" on shooting targets indicated the relative probability of a kill. Donovan developed the material several summers ago for his construction business. Now, he would use it for a completely different application. While his usual fare of mayhem included kidnapping, drug trafficking and murder, this mission would be altered in order to gain higher access, using lower resources, reaching into deeper pockets, for shallower reasons.

Little Abigail would soon be part incendiary device, part mule, but a full-strength terrorist conduit aimed at the one of the greatest leaders in the most powerful city in the world. A man who crossed another...one too many times. And Donovan Blair, aka Scorpion, would bite back with an explosive sting this city would never forget.

28.

KNUCKLE DOWN - CHAPTER 1

The end of my last mission didn't go exactly as I had imagined. To be perfectly honest, it went kinda sideways. And while my father Randall and his best friend and business partner Tony Black made it out of Cuba alive, they were certainly different. They would both be taking some much needed time off to let their old bodies heal. They were in good health, considering their age; however, what they had recently endured was a bit much for anyone. Randall will recover and heal nicely from a scorpion bite, thanks to Dr. Leonard Caprese. Once thought to be a traitor and perhaps an untrustworthy foe, Caprese did save my father's life. And just in the nick of time. As for Tony Black, the wound from Caprese's 9mm round he shot into Black's foot, ended up not being as bad as we originally thought. Black was one tough SOB and he knew how to play the drama. Luckily, or by design, Caprese had the foresight to aim at the end of his foot, rather than the middle, or near the ankle. What this meant was that Tony suffered a bone fracture, but in a few weeks will be as good as new. He may suffer a limp for several months, but he won't lose the foot. We understood now that Caprese had to display this showmanship, in order for him to earn Donovan's trust. Caprese needed to prove he had no vested interest in helping "the good guys." As for Donovan, aka "The Scorpion," unfortunately, he escaped our reach by mere seconds. And while he is a certifiable maniac, as one of the heaviest leaders in the drug and arms trafficking Underground, he didn't kill any of us. I suppose we have that to be thankful for. You could be sure I would spend the next several weeks, if not months, hot on his trail, with every intention of making him my next target. The time would soon come to pull out "Wilson," my trusty Cheytac rifle; otherwise, known as a sniper's wet dream.

As for the remaining good guys, Xeon disappeared to one of her favorite mountain retreats to catch up on some R & R. She didn't tell us where that secret spot was, nor with whom she would be sharing time, but it wouldn't be hard for me to find her when I needed. She was a true soldier, with a very bright future ahead. Peter Cohen returned to Key West, where he returned to his helicopter tour business. He said he'd seen enough "action" for awhile and preferred to lay low, sipping splashy cocktails and flirting with tourists who wanted to see the Keys from above.

Last but not least was my best pal, Mack. Whitestone demanded he take an official leave of absence in order to have his eye tended to. He was in line to have the very best care by the top surgeon in the business. Fortunately, that specialist, based at the Bascom Palmer Eye Institute in Miami, placed Mack not far from my dad's home. Like it or not, that would give Mack a regular visitor and Pops something to do while he recovered. Doctors said Mack suffered a detached retina from the gorilla who nearly knocked his eye out with the butt of a rifle, but would be fine in a few weeks. During his healing phase, I was going to enjoy teasing him about his Captain Hook eyepatch.

It was good to be back home at my mountain retreat outside Asheville. I was just about to venture out for a long hike with my trusty companion, Samson. I needed to clear my head and give my shoulder some time to heal from the gunshot wound I got in Havana. The screen door of my rustic cabin hadn't even finished slamming, when my cell rang. That ring was specific to only three people: Mack, Dad and Jerry, the commanding officer for all my "under the radar jobs." When Whitestone took over, I included him in the club. That ring generally meant trouble; either for me, or someone about to run into me. Given everyone had strict orders not to bother me for a good 72 hours, I assumed it was either an emergency with dad, which was doubtful, or from Mack. I was sure it wasn't him. That left Whitestone.

While I could have easily said I didn't hear the ring, or that I was out hiking with my dog, my gut told me I needed to answer it. Whistling for Samson, I motioned for him to sit and wait. As much as I didn't want to take the call, I did. Answering it, I knew instantly my life was about to take another turn. Within seconds of hearing

Whitestone's voice, along with the details of my next mission, I hung up, nearly threw up, then proceeded to pack up any thoughts of a long hike. Instead, I began prepping my Go-Bag for the next mission. My hunch was that it would be a long time before I'd be able to take that hike. This next case was important, not only to the powerful and most well-respected man I knew, but to me because once again it just got personal. And I had no time to waste.

KNUCKLE DOWN

David Temple's next novel in the Carter Matheson Series

COMING MAY 2016

David Temple has a natural talent for spinning words with novel catch-phrases and an uncanny ear for dialogue that makes his characters leap from the page. As an accomplished novelist, actor & filmmaker, it is obvious to see why David loves the art of story.

David's work spans multiple mediums and genres. He successfully developed his first novel, *Discovering Grace,* into the feature film, *Chasing Grace,* which was picked up and will be released by Word Films in 2016. The sequel to that book is the novel, *Stealing Hope*, which also has plans to be adapted to screen.

Behind The 8 Ball is the sequel to *Lucky Strikes*, the debut book in the Carter Matheson Series, which was released in 2015. Stay tuned for the next episode as Carter "Lucky" Matheson attempts to *KNUCKLE DOWN* in search of America's most notorious bad guys.

TWEET@davetemple + SURF@davidtemple.tv + FB@davidetemple

BOOK DESCRIPTION

CARTER MATHESON IS BACK. He and best pal Mack return from their last mission with barely enough time to unpack, when Washington calls on them to carry out another job. Lt. Colonel "Bulldog" Matheson and bodyguard Mr. Black have been kidnapped, and it's Carter & Mack's mission to bring them home. The high-stakes action heats up in Havanna, Cuba, where the legendary Dr. Leonard Caprese has infiltrated The Underground with a drug & arms dealer known as "The Scorpion." The clock is ticking. Suspense is building. And lives are on the line as money, drugs and power form the divide between good and evil. Dangerous men with dark intentions threaten not only the lives of Carter and his crew, but our national security.

www.ingramcontent.com/pod-product-compliance
Lightning Source LLC
Chambersburg PA
CBHW060212180626
46813CB00007B/2794

9780989186575